Miss Gipson Regrets She's Unable to Lunch Today. . . .

Jerry switched on more lights in a small office at the end of the corridor. He waved at it and sat down in a chair.

"Miss Gipson's," he said. "Her copies of her notes are in the lower right-hand drawer of the desk. . . ."

Pam North looked in the lower right-hand drawer of the desk. Then she looked at Jerry.

"I'm sorry, Jerry," she said, "but you did say 'right'? Because they aren't, you know."

"They were," he said. "I suppose she moved them. Look, darling."

"Listen, Jerry," she said. "Are you sure this is the right office? Because there's nothing in the desk. Nothing at all. . . ."

"We were late," Pam said. "In spite of everything, we were late."

Jerry nodded. He said there had evidently been something in Miss Gipson's desk that somebody wanted.

"Her murderer," Pam said.

"You jump, Pam," Jerry said. "But probably her murderer."

Books by Frances and Richard Lockridge

Murder Comes First
Murder Within Murder

Published by POCKET BOOKS

MURDER
WITHIN
MURDER

RICHARD AND
FRANCES LOCKRIDGE

PUBLISHED BY POCKET BOOKS NEW YORK

POCKET BOOKS, a Simon & Schuster division of
GULF & WESTERN CORPORATION
1230 Avenue of the Americas, New York, N.Y. 10020

ISBN: 0-671-44334-8

First Pocket Books printing July, 1982

10 9 8 7 6 5 4 3 2

POCKET and colophon are registered trademarks
of Simon & Schuster.

Printed in the U.S.A.

MURDER
WITHIN
MURDER

1

Miss Amelia Gipson presented a firm front to the world; she stood for no nonsense. For the conscious period of her fifty-two years she had stood for no nonsense in a world which was stubbornly nonsensical. The nonsense in the world had not been greatly abated by her attitude, but Miss Gipson's skirts were clean. What one person could do, she had done. If that was inadequate, the fault lay elsewhere; there was a laxity in higher places. Miss Gipson often suspected that there was.

She wore a gray rayon dress on this, the last evening of her life. It was fitted smoothly on her substantial body, which, although Miss Gipson was not notably a large woman, was apt to give frailer persons an impression of massiveness. It followed her firm bosom— a meticulously undivided expanse—with discretion; it was snug over her corseted hips. There was a touch of white at the throat; there was a little watch hanging from a silver pin on the left side of the central expanse. Above the touch of white at the throat, Miss Gipson's face was firm and untroubled; it was a face on which assurance rode, sure of a welcome. Miss Gipson did not know that it was the last evening of her life. Nothing was further from her thoughts.

The elevator man in the Holborn Annex greeted her with docile respect and rather as if he expected her to

7

smell his breath. She had complained to the management on one occasion that there had been, in George's car, an unmistakable odor of liquor. She had indicated a belief that it might have had its origin in George. She had pointed out that an elevator operated by a person under the influence of alcohol was a menace to the tenants. The management had listened, nodding agreement, and had taken it up.

"Beer ain't liquor," George had insisted. "I had me a beer. A beer ain't liquor."

Anything was liquor to Miss Gipson, the management thought, fleetingly, and as it thought of Miss Gipson had a sudden, unaccountable longing for a drink. But the management merely cautioned George, a little vaguely, not to let it happen again. He hoped, this evening, that Miss Gipson would not detect that it had happened again.

Miss Gipson was not thinking of George. She had collected her mail at the desk when she came in, and the top letter was addressed to Miss Amelia Gibson. Miss Gipson's eyes had hardened when she saw this, and realized that the world was at its nonsense again. There was no reason why the world, including department stores with fur collections to announce, should not learn that Miss Gipson's name was spelled with a *p*, instead of a common *b*. Miss Gipson had had a good deal of trouble with the world about this and resignedly expected to have more. It was not that she did not make the difference clear.

"Gip-son," she had always said, with the clearest possible enunciation. "With a *P*, not a *B*, *Gip-son*."

But the world was slovenly. To the world, Gipson sounded very like Gibson, and Gibson was easier. So Miss Gipson was, except by those who knew her best, almost always incorrectly addressed, and this did nothing to lessen her conviction that things were, in general, very badly run. They had been badly run as long as she could remember, and her memory started, with clarity, at the age of five. Of late years, things had been worse run than before, if anything.

"Good evening," Miss Gipson said to George, automatically and without sniffing. She said nothing more and George said nothing more until the car stopped at the tenth floor of the Holborn Annex. Miss Gipson stepped firmly out and went firmly down the corridor—down the middle of the corridor—to her door. She opened it and went in to her one-room furnished apartment, with bath, and laid her letters on the coffee table—from which Miss Gipson never drank coffee—which was in front of the sofa, on which Miss Gipson never lounged. She took off her hat and put it on the closet shelf and went to the bathroom and washed her face in lukewarm water. She dried her face and did not examine it further, knowing what it looked like. She washed her hands. She went back and sat down, erectly, on the sofa and opened her letters, beginning with the first one. She looked at it, sniffed— Miss Gipson did not wear furs, and disapproved of those who did—put it back in its envelope and laid it on the coffee table. She laid it so that it squared with the oblong of the table. She picked up the next letter.

It was correctly addressed. It began: "Dear Aunt Amelia." The writing of the letter was almost like printing; to it there was a certain flagrance, a kind of impertinence. But the content of the letter was straight-forward, almost blunt. Miss Gipson read it and sat for a moment looking at it.

"Well!" Miss Gipson said to herself. "She will, will she? Nonsense!"

Miss Gipson read the letter again, and smiled a little. She looked at the postmark and smiled again. By this time Nora would have got her letter; by this time Nora would know better, as she should have known from the beginning. That nonsense was going to end; that nonsense had, in fact, ended. No niece of hers. . . . Miss Gipson let the thought go unfinished. She took up the next letter. It, also, was correctly addressed. It began: "Dear Amelia." Miss Gipson read it and her eyes narrowed. She read it again and put it down on her lap and looked at the opposite wall without seeing it clearly. It was as if she were looking through the opposite wall out into a world full of nonsense—

reprehensible nonsense. Miss Gipson's face was not expressive, and there was no one there to attempt its reading. But it was for a moment troubled; for a moment confidence was uneasy on it. There was more than one kind of nonsense in the world, Miss Gipson thought.

"But," she reminded herself, "there are more ways than one of killing a cat, too."

She put the letter down on top of the one which began "Dear Aunt Amelia" and opened her fourth letter. She merely glanced at it and put it down on the letter advertising furs. She made it expressly clear that she had no intention of paying good money for unsatisfactory merchandise, war or no war. If storekeepers chose to disregard her irrefutable statements, the responsibility—and the inevitable chagrin—were theirs. Miss Gipson's position had been stated.

She sat for a moment and then picked up the letter which began "Dear Amelia" and read it again. She also read again the letter from Nora. Then she put these two letters in a pigeonhole of a small secretary. She put the other two letters in a wastebasket, after tearing them twice across. She thought a moment, took out the letter which had contained a bill she had no intention of paying, and tore it into even, small fragments. It was entirely possible that the maid who cleaned the room read letters thrown into the wastebasket, piecing them together like crossword puzzles. There was, certainly, little to indicate that she did much else in the room. Miss Gipson absently ran a finger along the writing shelf of the secretary and looked at it. She made a small, disparaging sound with her tongue and teeth. Nonsense! War or no war, an apartment hotel like the Annex could manage to get proper help. The management was shiftless and indifferent. It permitted chambermaids not only to neglect their jobs, but to wear perfume while doing it. Miss Gipson sniffed. More than usual, this time, and a new brand. No improvement, however; there were no gradations in perfume, so far as Miss Gipson could tell. All represented laxity, at the best. At the worst they were invitations to the most nonsensical of human activities. It was an activity in which Miss Gipson had never had a part, and which—she hardly needed to assure herself—she had no interest. Wherein, it had to be admitted, she differed from far too much of the world. Miss Gipson had no illusion that the particular nonsense to which perfume—and so much else you could see and hear and in other fashions not ignore—invited, was of limited scope. Miss Gipson saw it, in its secondary manifestations, to be sure, everywhere. She had disapproved of it since she was ten; her disapproval had never faltered.

"Chambermaids!" Miss Gipson thought. "Boys, nothing but boys. And Nora."

Miss Gipson would not have spoken thus scatteredly. Her conversation was never scattered. But her thoughts, as she so often had occasion to point out, were her own.

She looked at her watch. It told her the time was ten minutes of six. Then the telephone rang.

"Miss Gipson speaking," she said, as soon as she picked up the telephone. She waited a moment for the inevitable readjustment to take place. "*This* is Miss Gipson," she said. She said it in the tone of forbearance she had used so often when she had a desk of her own at the college, before it became necessary for her to resign because nonsense—and worse than nonsense—was so widespread even at Ward; before it was clear that, even there, the moral laxity which was demoralizing the world was creeping in. Not that the world's morality, even at its best, had ever met Miss Gipson's standards.

"Yes, John?" Miss Gipson said into the telephone. Her tone was not inviting. She listened.

"There is no reason for any further discussion," she said. "And in any case, I am occupied this evening."

She listened again.

"There is no use going over that again, John," she said. "I am perfectly aware that it says at my discretion. I am exercising my discretion. Mr. Backley entirely agrees."

She listened again, briefly.

"I can only advise patience, John," she said. "It is an excellent virtue. I am sure my dear brother meant you to learn patience when he made his very wise arrangements about you and your sister."

She listened again.

"About that, also, I must exercise my discretion," she said. "You can tell your sister so. I have already told her. She cannot expect me to be a party to what I consider immorality."

The answer was apparently only a word or two—perhaps only a word.

"Immorality," Amelia Gipson repeated, without emotion. "I call it what it is. Nora cannot expect me to countenance any such action. I shall certainly make the situation clear to the person concerned if she makes it necessary. I've told her that."

She listened again, for the last time.

"I do not care if I am the only person in the world who takes what you call that attitude," she said. "So much the worse for the world. Right is right, John. Goodbye."

She hung up. She nodded her head slightly, approving herself. She looked at her watch. It was six o'clock. She shook her head in slight annoyance over that. She got her hat from the closet and put it on without consulting a mirror. She checked the contents of her orderly handbag. She looked around the orderly room and left it, locking the door behind her. She had insisted on a special lock, which she could make sure of with her own key.

George was no longer on the elevator. There was a girl operating it and there was a faint scent of perfume in the car; it was not, Miss Gipson thought, the same scent she had noticed in her apartment. Otherwise she would have thought that this was the chambermaid on her floor. The girl said "good evening" and Miss Gipson slightly inclined her head without replying. She would not encourage the nonsense of girls as elevator operators.

The doorman also said "good evening" to Miss

Gipson. She replied to him, in a clear, decisive voice which did not invite further conversation. She walked up the street to the square and the doorman looked after her and, as she turned the corner, raised his shoulders just perceptibly and for his own amusement. Quite an old girl, the doorman thought. Glad he wasn't married to her. Then he realized that was an odd thought to have in relation to Miss Gipson, although it had no doubt been widely held.

It was ten after six when Miss Gipson sat down to dinner in a tearoom near Washington Square. It was called the Green House and the door was painted green and there were ferns in the window. The waitress put the usual peg under one of the legs of Miss Gipson's table to steady it and said they had a few lamb chops and it was lucky Miss Gipson had not been a few minutes later. Miss Gipson had a lamb chop, very well done, and creamed potatoes, string beans and a salad of two slices of tomato and a lettuce leaf with a rather sour dressing. She had a piece of cocoanut cake and a cup of tea, and caught an uptown Fifth Avenue bus at a few minutes before seven.

It was twenty minutes past seven when Miss Gipson entered the New York Public Library for the last time. Since she had been working regularly at the Library for several weeks and had worked close to schedule during afternoons and evenings, it was subsequently possible to trace her movements with fair exactitude. She had entered one of the elevators at around seven thirty or a little before, and had got off at the third floor. She had turned in slips for "Famous American Murders," by Algernon Bentley; "The Trial of Martha West," one of the Famous Trials series; and for magazine articles on the unsolved murder of Lorraine Purdy—unsolved largely because of the disappearance of Frank Purdy, whom Lorraine had unwisely married—and the presumably solved domestic crime wave which had taken off the elderly Mrs. William Rogers and her daughter, Susan, together with a maid who had unwisely eaten what remained of some chicken à la king which had been prepared primarily for Mrs. Rogers but had been, in the end, rather too widely distributed. Mrs. Rogers' nephew had been suspected of adding an unorthodox ingredient to the chicken à la king, but there had been other possibilities. The nephew, whose name was Samuel King, had been somewhat halfheartedly convicted by a jury, which resolved its doubts by bringing in a second-degree verdict, to the freely expressed annoyance of Justice Ryerson.

Amelia Gipson had received the books and the bound volumes of the magazines in which the articles appeared in the North Reading Room. At about nine o'clock, or a few minutes later, she had been seen by one of the attendants leaving the catalogue room through the main door. A few minutes later she had returned. She had been absent about long enough to walk to a drinking fountain down the corridor, the attendant thought.

At a quarter of ten, fifteen minutes before the library closed, Miss Gipson became violently ill at her seat at one of the long tables. She died in the emergency ward of Bellevue Hospital at about eleven o'clock. Sodium fluoride poisoning had been diagnosed promptly; but Miss Gipson had not responded to treatment.

2

Mr. North was reading a manuscript and the word *No* was slowly forming itself in his mind when the whirring started. At first it was not clearly identifiable as a whirring. It was more a kind of buzzing. It might, Jerry North thought, even be in his head. Exhaustion, possibly. Or the manuscript. He shook his head, thinking the sound might go away, and dug back into the manuscript. "It must be admitted," the manuscript said, "that in the post-war world we face an increasing agglomeration of—" Clearly, Jerry North decided, it was the manuscript. The post-war world was buzzing at him. Its shining machinery, made to a large degree out of plastic, was whirring at unimagined tasks, turning out things made largely of glass. Whatever the post-war world might finally be, it would inevitably also be a buzzing in the ears.

He put down the manuscript and covered his eyes with a hand and waited for this audible omen of the future to go away. It did not go away. It came into the living room and sat down on the sofa. If it was in his head, there was something drastically wrong with his head. A little fearfully, Mr. North parted his fingers and looked at the sofa, on which the future sat, buzzing. The future was Mrs. North, wearing an apron over a very short play suit. The future, Jerry North decided, was brighter than he had allowed himself to

15

hope. The future was Pamela North in a checked apron over a brief play suit, with a bowl in its lap and an egg beater in its hands.

Jerry smiled at his wife, who stared into the bowl with fixed interest. A cake, Jerry decided, vaguely. It was an odd time to be making a cake. Ten o'clock—no, five after ten—in the evening was an odd time to make a cake. But when Pam made cakes—and when she made pies, as she sometimes did, and once doughnuts—it was apt to be at odd times. She had made doughnuts at an odd time, the only time she had made doughnuts. They had been to the theater and, waiting for a cab, had stepped for shelter under the awning of a store in which they were making doughnuts and serving them to people, apparently to advertise a brand of coffee. Pam had said nothing then, but when she had got home she had said suddenly that what she was hungry for was doughnuts, and why not make some? They had made some and they were fine, but Pam had somehow mis-estimated, because there were more doughnuts than, from the ingredients involved, seemed conceivable. They had made doughnuts until after two in the morning, taking turns frying them, and by that time everything in the house was full of doughnuts and so were the Norths. They were full of doughnuts for several days and after that they were not much interested in doughtnuts for a long time, and never again in making them. That, of course, was pre-war; post-war would unquestionably be different. There would, Mr. North thought, eyeing the manuscript, be little room for doughnuts in the post-war world.

"Hmmm!" Pam said. Jerry looked at her and she was looking into the bowl and had stopped turning the egg beater. He deduced that the sound, which had not really so much form even as "hmmm," invited him to conversation.

"Cake?" he said, by way of conversation.

"As far as I can see," Pam North said, "it's whipped cream and always will be. Of course not, Jerry! At ten o'clock at night?"

"Not a cake," Jerry said. He thought. "Pie?" he said, a little hopefully.

"You don't beat a pie," Pam said. "And it would still be ten o'clock at night, wouldn't it?"

"I see what you mean," Jerry said.

"Butter," Pam said. "Only it isn't. And it's *been* half an hour. Or almost."

"Butter?" Jerry said.

Pam said of course butter. What did he think?

"Well," Jerry said. "I didn't think butter. I thought we didn't have any butter. I thought you had spent your red points up through December."

"November," Mrs. North said. "It's very nice of Morris, but sometimes I think it's illegal. Do you suppose it is?"

Jerry said he supposed it was, in a fairly mild way. But it all came out pretty much the same in the end.

"Except," Pam said, "when they end it we'll be ahead, you know. And where will Morris be?"

Morris, Mr. North thought, would be all right.

"Anyway," Pam said, "there wasn't any other way I could think of, and he said it was all right to take them in advance. Of course, it would be different if we had children. It's different for people with children. Particularly babies." Mrs. North resumed grinding the egg beater. "Babies really pay off," she said. "Nothing but milk, or blue points at the worst. Before they abolished them."

"Listen," Jerry said, pulling himself away from the idea that someone had abolished babies. "What about butter? I thought you couldn't use any more butter. I thought it was straight olive oil from here on in."

"Of course we can't use butter," Pam said. "That's why I'm making it."

"You're—" Jerry said and paused—"you're making butter?"

"Why not?" Pam said. "Only apparently I'm not. It's still whipped cream. And they told me it wouldn't be more than half an hour."

"You mean," Jerry said, "that you're sitting there, in a play suit, making butter? *Butter?*"

"Of course," Pam said. "Churning, really. You take some cream—except the cream's so thin now you have to take the top of milk, except the milk's pretty thin too—and beat it until it's butter. If ever, which I doubt. Here, you churn."

She lifted the bowl from her lap and held it toward Jerry, who got up and went over to the sofa and sat down beside her and looked into the bowl. It was full of whipped cream, sure enough. He said so. He said it just looked like whipped cream to him.

"Although come to think of it," he said, "my mother used to say to look out it didn't turn to butter. That was when I was a boy, of course."

"Well," Pam said. "There still is butter, even if you aren't a boy. And everybody says it will work. Beat, Jerry!"

Jerry beat. He held the egg beater in his left hand and twirled with his right and the beater made a deep, intricate swirl in the soft, yellowish whipped cream.

"You know," Jerry said, after a while, "I never thought we'd be churning here in a New York apartment. Ten floors up, particularly. Did you?"

Pam said it was the war. The war had changed a lot of things and the changes had outlasted it. They both looked into the bowl, trying to see the future in it. Then Pam spoke, suddenly.

"Jerry!" she said. "You're spattering!"

"I—" Jerry began, and stopped. He was certainly spattering. Because, as suddenly as Pam had spoken, the whipped cream had come apart. Part of it was thin and spattering and part of it—

"For God's sake!" Jerry said, in a shocked voice. "Butter!"

It was butter. It was sticking to the egg beater. There was not a great deal of it. It was not exactly a solid. But it was beyond doubt butter. The Norths looked at one another with surprise and delight and disbelief.

"Jerry!" Pam said. *"We made butter!"*

"I know," Jerry said. "It's like—like finding gold. Or a good manuscript. It's—it's very strange."

They took the bowl out to the kitchen and scraped the butter off the egg beater and poured off what they supposed was buttermilk—although it didn't taste like buttermilk—and squeezed the water out of the butter as Pam had been told to do. And they were wrapping up almost a quarter of a pound of butter in oiled paper, and still not really believing it, when the telephone rang. Pam was wrapping, and thereupon wrapped more intently, so Jerry was stuck with the telephone.

The voice on the telephone was familiar, and Jerry said, "Yes, Bill?" When she heard him, Pamela put the butter into the icebox quickly and came in and stood in front of Jerry and made faces until he noticed her. Jerry said, "Wait a minute, Bill," and when he looked at her Pam spoke.

"Tell him we made butter," she said. "Tell him he's the first to know."

"Pam says we made butter, Bill," Jerry said. "We did, too. Almost a quarter of a pound."

He listened.

"What did he say?" Pam said.

"He said 'well,' " Jerry told her.

"Was he excited?" Pam wanted to know.

"Were you excited, Bill?" Jerry said into the telephone. Then he spoke to Pam. "He says 'reasonably,' " Jerry told her. "But he says he's got a murder if we don't mind."

"Oh," Pam said. "All right. Tell him we're sorry."

"Pam says we're sorry, Bill," Jerry said into the telephone. "What?"

His voice was suddenly different and, as she heard the change, Pam's own expressive face was shadowed. Because something Bill had said had made murder real to Jerry, and that would make it real to her. She did not want murder to be real again—not ever again.

"Yes," he said. "A woman fiftyish—solidly built—gray hair? With a *p* instead of a *b* as it happens. Yes She's been working for us. At the office. Research."

He listened for almost a minute and there was a

queer expression on his face. Then he seemed to break in.

"I can explain that," he said. "She was doing research for us—preliminary research. For a book we're getting out on the subject. Do you want the details?"

He listened again.

"Naturally," he said. "She has relatives in the city, I think. But I'll come around. Although from what you say there doesn't seem to be much doubt."

He listened again.

"All right," he said. "The morgue. I'll be along."

He replaced the receiver and looked at Pam a moment, his thoughts far from her. Then he brought them back.

"A woman named Amelia Gipson," he said. "She was working at the office—had been for about a month. Somebody seems to have poisoned her. In the Public Library, of all places. Bill wants me to make a preliminary identification before he gets in touch with her relatives."

"In the Public Library?" Pam said. "At Forty-second Street? The big one?"

Jerry nodded.

"What a strange place," Pam North said. "It's—it's always so quiet there."

"Yes," Jerry said. "She was reading about murders at the time, apparently. For us. For the murder book I told you about. *My Favorite Murder*—working title. Remember?"

Pam said she remembered. With a writer for each crime—a writer who wrote about murder. She remembered.

"Miss Gipson was getting together preliminary data," Jerry said. "We promised them that. It was an odd job for her, come to think of it, She used to be a college professor—or something like it. Anyway, she used to teach in a college. She was a trained researcher. But it was an odd job for her."

It ended oddly enough, Pam thought, and said. It ended very oddly.

"I think I'll go with you," Pam said then. "It's so strange about its being the Public Library."

Jerry thought she shouldn't, but she did.

The body was under a sheet and they pulled the sheet back from the face. Confidence no longer sat on the face; the features were twisted, curiously. But it was Amelia Gipson and Jerry turned to Lieut. William Weigand of Homicide and nodded.

"What?" Jerry said. "And how?"

Bill Weigand told him what.

"I don't know how," he said. "Suddenly, sitting in the Library, she was very sick. As she would be. Then in about an hour she was dead. In Bellevue. That's all we know, at the moment."

"You don't eat anything in the Library," Pam pointed out. "Do you?"

Bill smiled faintly and shook his head. That was it, he said; that was part of it. Unless you were on the staff, you didn't eat in the Library. You didn't drink.

"So," Jerry pointed out, "she had taken it—had been given it—before she went to the Library."

Bill Weigand shook his head. He said the time didn't fit. He said she had been at the Library for something like two hours—probably more—when she became ill.

"It doesn't wait that long," he said. "We've established that. The dose she seems to have got would have made her violently ill in half an hour or so. Her book slips were time stamped at 7:33. Allow her some time to find the books she wanted in the catalogues, fill out the slips—say a quarter of an hour—and we have her in the Library at fifteen after seven, or thereabouts. Of course, she may have left the Library and come back. If she didn't, she was poisoned in the Library. Presumably while she was sitting at one of the tables in the reading room—the North Reading Room."

"You mean," Pam said, "somebody just came along and said 'Sorry to interrupt your reading, but do you mind drinking some poison?' Because I don't believe it."

"Not that way, obviously," Jerry said. "You're getting jumpy, Pam."

"Not any way like it that I can see," Pam said. "And I'm not getting jumpy. Do you, Bill?"

Practice helped. Bill did not even have to check back to the clause before the clause.

"It doesn't seem possible," he said. "And it happened. Therefore—a job for us. For Deputy Chief Inspector Artemus O'Malley and his helpers. Mullins. Stein. Me."

"Well," Pam said. "She worked in Jerry's office." It was merely statement; it held implications.

Mullins was in the shadows. Mullins spoke.

"O'Malley won't like it, loot," Mullins said. "He sure as hell won't like it. He likes 'em kept simple."

"But," Pam said, "it isn't simple. Hello, Sergeant Mullins. Is it?"

"Hello, Mrs. North," Mullins said. "No. But the inspector don't want you in none of them. None. He says you *make* 'em complicated. Hard, sort of."

"All right, sergeant," Bill Weigand said, and there was only the thin edge of amusement in his voice. "She was an employee of Mr. North. It was inevitable that we call him. For the moment—until we get in touch with her relatives—we can assume he represents her interests. Right?"

"Say," Mullins said. "That's right, ain't it, loot?"

"Of course it is," Pam said. "Where do we go, Bill? First?"

Bill shrugged. There were a hundred directions. The Library. The office of North Books, Inc. Amelia Gipson's apartment.

"Mullins is going to the Library," he said. "Stein's there, and some of the boys. I'm going to the apartment." He paused and smiled a little. "I should think," he said, "that Jerry has a right to accompany me, Pam."

"So should I," Pam North said. "Shall we start now? It isn't—it isn't very nice in here." She looked around the morgue. "It never is," she said, thoughtfully.

While Bill Weigand picked up a parcel containing Miss Gipson's handbag, and signed a receipt for it, and while they got into the big police car Pam had been silent. Now, as they started toward Washington Square and the Holborn Annex she spoke.

"Why," Pam said, "didn't she kill herself?"

"Miss Gipson?" Jerry said, in a startled voice. "She would no more. . . ." Then he broke off and looked at Bill. "Which is true," he said, after a moment. "She wouldn't think of it—wouldn't have thought of it. But you didn't know that, Bill. How did you know?"

Bill nodded. He said he had been wondering why they didn't ask him that.

"That's the way Inspector O'Malley wanted it," he said. "That's the way he thinks it ought to be. Simple. Suicide. Unfortunately, she wrote us a note."

"What kind of a note?" Pam said. "Non-suicide note?"

Weigand looked at Pam North with approval. He said, "Right."

"She was taking notes," he said. "On the Purdy murder. Writing them out very carefully in a notebook, in ink—very carefully and clearly. And we almost missed her note to us—did miss it the first time. Then Stein thought that while the last thing she had written almost fitted, it didn't really fit. The last thing she wrote was: 'I have been poisoned by—! It didn't finish. Just 'I have been poisoned by—' and a scraggly line running off the page."

"Then how," Pam said, "can even—can the inspector think it was suicide. If he still does."

Bill Weigand said the inspector still wanted to.

"And," he said, "he can make a talking point. You see, she was taking notes on a poison case. The death of a woman named Lorraine Purdy, who was killed, curiously enough, with sodium fluoride. Presumably by her husband, although we were supposed to think by accident. But it wasn't accident—it was Purdy. He ran for it and got himself killed in an airplane accident. O'Malley wants to think that the last thing Miss Gipson wrote was part of her notes on the Purdy case."

He smiled faintly.

"We can't let him," he said. "It almost fits. It doesn't fit. Why was she taking notes on the Purdy case, Jerry?"

Jerry explained that. It was not only the Purdy case. It was a series of cases—ten murder cases, all famous, all American. Her notes were to go to selected writers who were accepted as specialists in crime. "Like Edmund Pearson was," Jerry amplified. Each was to write the story of one of the murders as a chapter in a book. Jerry was to publish the book. It had been his idea. It was not, he added, a new idea. Other publishers had done it; he had done it before himself, several years earlier. There was always a market for crime. As Pearson had proved; as Woollcott had proved; as dozens of lesser writers had proved.

"We did the digging for them," Jerry said. "Miss Gipson did the digging for us. She was a researcher."

When he decided on publishing the book and had needed somebody to do research, Jerry had decided against tying up anybody on his own staff—a rather small staff these days—on a long and detailed job. He had gone to a college placement bureau and Miss Gipson was the result. The rather unexpected result.

"I'd supposed we'd get a girl just out of college," Jerry North said. "Most of them are—the research girls. Miss Gipson was a surprise. She'd been a Latin teacher in a small, very good college for girls in Indiana—Ward College, I think it was. She got tired of it or something and decided on a new field. She was a little surprised when it turned out to be murder research, but she was doing a good job."

"I think," Pam said, "she carried it too far."

They looked at her.

"I only mean," she said, "you don't have to go to the length of getting murdered. It's too—thorough."

The two men looked at each other and after a while Jerry said "oh."

3

You started with a body and tried to bring life back to it, Pam thought, looking around the room in which Miss Gipson had lived. That was what you did in murder—that was what Bill Weigand had to do. She looked at him, standing in the middle of the room and looking around it, his eyes quick. He was building—trying to build—in his own mind the person who had been Amelia Gipson. He started with the body of a middle-aged woman; a body growing cold on a slab in the morgue; a body which said certain things, but not enough. The body spoke of regular meals, of comfortable life, of the number of years lived, of the manner of death. It told—it would tell—what the last meal eaten by a living person had been, and how long it had been eaten before death. It told of past illnesses which had been endured and survived; of an appendicitis operation many years before; of virginity maintained until it withered.

Those things the body in the morgue told of. But they were not the things which were most significant; which now were most vital. The body could not tell who had hated Amelia Gipson, or if anyone had loved her; it could not tell what she thought of things, and what others thought of her—of her tastes, her needs, her responsibilities. It could not tell where, in her life, had sprouted the seed of her death. These things—all the things Bill Weigand had to find out—lay now in the

25

little things Amelia Gipson had left behind. They lay in this room, and its order; in the letters and notebooks and check-stubs in the secretary in the corner; in what men and women had seen and remembered about Miss Gipson that evening; in the contents of her medicine cabinet and her safe deposit box, if she had one. The things they had to know lay in what she had done in the past and what she had planned to do in the future. Research into death was at the same time research into life.

"She used scent," Pam said, suddenly. "Does that surprise you? Either of you?"

"No," Jerry said. "I don't think she used perfume, Pam. I didn't notice it at the office."

"You must have had a cold," Pam said. "You didn't mention it."

"I didn't have it," Jerry said.

Pam said all right. She said in that case it was because he smoked too much. Clearly, Miss Gipson had used perfume. It was still in the room.

"Right," Bill Weigand said. "I noticed it. But she didn't wear any tonight. I noticed that, too."

"Something with 'Fleur' in it," Pam said. "Fleur de Something or Other. Fleur de what?"

Neither of the men knew. But Jerry admitted there was perfume in the room.

"For evenings, probably," Pam said. "Although it doesn't seem in character, somehow. The way she looked. And being a Latin teacher in a girls' school. I'd have thought castile soap and perhaps a little talcum, if anything."

Bill Weigand had crossed to the desk. He was looking through it, piling the contents of pigeonholes in neat order. He had left Miss Gipson's purse lying on the coffee table. It was all right for her to look into it, Bill told Pam absently, when she asked.

It was a very neat purse. Pam thought that it was much neater than any purse she had ever looked into—certainly much neater than her own. And it seemed almost empty. There was a change purse in it, containing a little more than twenty dollars. There was a social security card. No driver's license. A fountain pen. Four neat squares of cleansing tissue. No compact. No lipstick. No lists of any kind, scrawled on the backs of envelopes. No scraps of material, no hairpins or loose stamps or unanswered correspondence. It was hardly recognizable as a woman's handbag.

"And no perfume," Pam said aloud. "In it or on it. Which is odd."

Bill Weigand was reading a letter and Jerry stood by him, reading over his shoulder. Pam got up, leaving the handbag, and went into the bathroom. It was a neat bathroom. She opened the built-in medicine cabinet. There was a box of bicarbonate and a plastic drinking cup, a box of cleansing tissue, two toothbrushes and a can of tooth powder, a can of white talcum with no perceptible scent and a carboard box from a druggist with a doctor's name on it and the handwritten instructions: "One powder three times a day two hours after meals." On a shelf inset under the medicine cabinet were a comb and brush and a box of hairpins. Nowhere that Pam could see was there any perfume.

Nowhere in the apartment, she found, was there any perfume, except that which faintly haunted the air. So it was not Miss Gipson's perfume, but had been worn by a guest. It was a tiny discovery and, having made it, Pam decided it was of no importance; that it was not even a discovery. Because the perfume had probably been worn by a chambermaid while she was cleaning up the room. Pam went over, satisfied, and stood beside Jerry, behind Bill Weigand.

"Find anything, Pam?" Bill said, without looking up from the letter he was reading.

"No," Pam said. "Except that she didn't wear perfume after all. It was a maid. Or somebody who came to see her. And she had indigestion. There are some powders in the medicine cabinet to be taken after meals. And there's nothing much in her purse."

There had been more in it, Bill told her. One other object—a folding aluminum cup.

"You mean," Pam said, "one of those things made of rings that catch on each other? They always leak and I haven't seen one for ages. I thought they went out when paper cups came in."

He meant that kind of a cup, Bill told her. He had not seen one for a long time either. But Miss Gipson had had one in her purse and it was now in the police laboratory, because—

"Bill!" Pam said, "Jerry! To take her medicine in when she was away from home. After meals. *Two hours after meals.* But tonight she was a little late. Only not late enough."

Bill Weigand put down the letter and turned to look at her and Jerry looked at her too. Then the two men looked at each other. Bill got up.

"In the medicine cabinet?" he said, and was already across the room to the bathroom door. He came out holding in a handkerchief the cardboard box of medicine, and they opened it on the coffee table. It was half filled with folded papers. He opened the paper nearest the front of the box and sniffed the powder it held. He looked a little disappointed.

"Smells like medicine," he said. "Not like sodium fluoride. But it is a little greenish."

He answered the enquiry in their looks. Sodium fluoride, he said, was colored green in accordance with a requirement of the State law, to minimize the risk of confusing it with some harmless powder—as once, in another state, it had been confused with baking powder with tragic results.

"What's it for, anyway?" Jerry asked, and Pam and Bill Weigand answered almost at once: "Roaches."

"That, by the way," Bill said, "was how we got on to Purdy—the guy Miss Gipson was reading about. The Purdys didn't have roaches. He'd forgotten that when he arranged for an accident to happen to his wife. The whole building had been fumigated about a week before they moved in—and they had just moved in when Mrs. Purdy died. Mr. Purdy would have had a spot of trouble explaining that when we sprung it on him at the trial. It was something we had up our sleeves."

As he talked, he opened another folded slip of paper

and sniffed the contents. He shook his head and tried a third and shook his head again. The he refolded the powder into the paper containers and put them back in the box.

"We need a chemist for this," he said. "It seems to be medicine. But—"

"But the one she took tonight needn't have been," Pam said. "Somebody could have filled one of these folders with poison and left it for her to take. Putting it in front, of course, where she would be sure to take it."

"Would she?" Jerry said.

Pam thought she would. She thought that Miss Gipson had done all things in due order and that, with folders of digestive powder—if it was digestive powder—filed neatly in a box she would as neatly have removed them, starting from the front.

"In character," Pam said. "But as a matter of fact, almost anybody would. It's the natural way to do it. So if somebody wanted Miss Gipson to die tonight, he would put a folder of sodium fluoride in front of the folders of medicine in the box and be pretty sure she would take it with her when she went out. Only—"

Only, Jerry pointed out, she might have carried a day's supply with her at a time. Or she might take them only irregularly; only when she needed them.

"But," he said, "there is nothing to indicate that it made any difference precisely when she died, is there Bill?"

Weigand, still looking at the box, shook his head. He said there was very little at the moment to indicate more than that Amelia Gipson was dead of poison and that, unless she had lied as the last action of her life, she had not killed herself.

"But," he said, "it's quite possible that somebody did put a folder of sodium fluoride in with Miss Gipson's medicine, figuring that she would take it sooner or later. If someone could get into the apartment and find the medicine—and knew she took it—it wouldn't be too difficult. And—"

"The perfume!" Pam said. "That's where it came

from. The murderer was wearing it. Which narrows things down to women, or almost."

"Almost?" Jerry repeated, and then, when Pam looked at him, said "oh."

"Either reading," Pam told him.

Bill urged her to keep it simple. He reminded her of Inspector O'Malley.

"Say it was a woman," he said. "And don't bank too much on the theory. It may have been the maid who cleaned up the room."

"Then," Pam said, "somebody's going to have to smell the maids. Not me. It was too embarrassing, before."*

Bill Weigand agreed, without excitement. He said he would have it checked. Tomorrow. Not by Pam North.

"But," she said, "how will somebody else know? That it's the same, I mean, or isn't, without smelling it. It won't last forever here, you know."

"One of us will have to remember the scent," he told her. "I'll have the boys bring in samples, if necessary. There probably aren't very many maids. They probably haven't been able to get very many maids."

"All right," Pam said. "What else? Here?"

There was, Weigand told her, a good deal else. Now he seemed more interested than he had before; it was as if he had been waiting to take up something more important. There were letters, he said. And bank records. He looked at Jerry curiously.

"Did you get the idea she needed a job?" he said. "That she needed it to live on?"

Jerry said he hadn't got any particular idea about it. He said that was the reason people usually got jobs. He added, thoughtfully, that he couldn't think of any other good reason.

"Well," Bill said, "she didn't need the job. For one thing, she had better than twenty thousand in a cash balance at the Corn Exchange. And three savings

---

* Pamela North attempted to smell out a murderer in "Payoff For The Banker" (J. B. Lippincott, 1945). She was widely misunderstood.

accounts each up to the seventy-five hundred maximum. And in addition she seems to have been custodian of a trust fund. Anyway she's got a book of checks printed up for the Alfred Gipson Trust and she's been signing as trustee. How much did you pay her, Jerry?"

"Forty," Jerry told him.

Bill Weigand raised his shoulders and let them fall. There, his shoulders said, was that.

"A discrepancy," Pam amplified.

Jerry said it was all of that. But Bill had picked up a small sheaf of letters.

Jerry said he had been wondering. Then they got to the letters. Pam held out her hand and Bill Weigand picked one of the letters from the little sheaf and handed it to her. She read:

"Dear Aunt Amelia: I'm not going to get down on my hands and knees any more about it. What you say you are going to do is wicked and barbaric—it's no better than murder. It's terrible that there are people like you in the world. You know I love Kennet—that I always loved him—that what you found out didn't make any difference. I think you want to kill that—what's between Kennet and me. Maybe you can. But don't think I won't try to stop you—every way there is."

The letter was signed only with a capital "N." It was a kind of proud and flaunting "N." The letter was written in a characteristic hand—decisive, clear; very vigorous and very young.

"Well!" Pam said. "She didn't like Aunt Amelia? Who is she?"

Apparently, Bill said, she was Nora Gipson, Amelia Gipson's niece. There was a reference to her in one of the other letters; a letter about the trust fund. Which did not, at the moment, seem to have any bearing. However—He handed Pam a second letter. It was written in a sloping, nervous hand that quavered a little. It was written also by a woman; by, if you accepted the heading on the letter paper, Mrs. Willard

Burt. It addressed itself to "Dear Amelia" and went on:

"You have made—somehow—a terrible mistake. You should know that what you think is impossible—if you really do think it. I keep feeling that I must have misunderstood you yesterday. It is the only thing I can think. That you could really imagine—dream—But I won't go on.

"Amelia, you used to know—in the old days—that you could trust me. Believe me, nothing has changed— I haven't changed. You can trust me now as you used to—trust me when I tell you that there is nothing— absolutely nothing—in what you say.

"Dear—I know this isn't very coherent. But we can't let things stay as they are. It isn't safe—for either of us. Won't you come and have lunch with me? On Thursday—here? I know if we can talk quietly I can make you understand how insanely wrong you are."

The letter was signed: "As ever, Helen."

Pam looked at the letter for a moment after she had finished it. Then, slowly, she read it again. Her face was puzzled.

"I don't understand it, do you?" she said. She might have been speaking to either of the men. "It's— pathetic. And somehow frightening. Or was she—this Helen—just sort of hysterical—about something not really as important as she thinks?"

Bill said he didn't know. He said it was one of the things they would have to find out. As they would have to find out about Nora. About the perfumed woman who substituted poison for medicinal powders. About the peculiar discrepancy between Amelia Gipson's apparently very comfortable financial situation and the forty-dollar-a-week job she had elected to take with North Books, Inc.

"About the job," Pam said. "Could she have found out something? About one of the old murders? Something that made her dangerous, even now?"

Bill Weigand thought for a moment, and then emphasized the doubt on his face by shaking his head. He said he shouldn't think so.

"You don't," he pointed out, "make some new discovery about an old crime by reading what newspaper and magazine writers—or even book writers, Jerry—say about it. Because the police always know more; much more. You know that. More even than the official records. It's in the minds of the men who have worked on the case—in their hunches—in what they've guessed from the look in somebody's eyes, in the tones of voices. Stuff that isn't written down. At best, people who write about old crimes have to rely on logic. And at best, logic isn't enough. Not in this business."

Pam said she knew. She said there was no doubt he was right. She said it was only an interesting coincidence.

"Anyway," Jerry pointed out, "the murders she was working on are, with one or two exceptions, solved murders. And the exceptions—as I remember them—go a good ways back. Somebody wanted to do the Hall-Mills case again, and I couldn't talk him out of it, although it's been done to death. But I shouldn't think Amelia would happen to stumble on a dangerous solution of that one. For one thing, almost everybody's dead."

Bill Weigand broke it up. He said that, in any event, they were done there. For the moment. Tomorrow they would really do the apartment. Tomorrow they would—and he smiled at that—have the chambermaids smelled by an expert smeller. He stood up and the Norths went ahead of him out of the apartment. At the door, Weigand bent and examined the lock. He stood up and said that people were fools.

"She's had a special lock put on," he said. "About half as good—as safe—as the one she had taken off, unless the builders skimped badly. I could open this one with a bent hairpin."

"Really?" Pam said, and looked at the lock in turn.

"No," Bill Weigand said. "Maybe not. But I could open it with a pick in a couple of minutes; an expert could do it in thirty seconds. And anybody, with a reasonable assortment of keys, would have a ten-to-one chance of simply walking in."

They went down the hall, and down to the desk in the lobby. Weigand telephoned the precinct for a man to stand by outside Miss Gipson's apartment until the next day; he spoke briefly to the sleepy manager of the Holborn Annex. He arranged for the questioning, the next morning, of the maid who did the rooms on Miss Gipson's floor; he discovered that maid service was optional with the tenants, and that by no means all of them wanted it, and that as a result there were only three women—one of them young, the other two middle-aged—employed regularly by the Annex. The younger woman did Miss Gipson's room.

He spoke about the lock, and the manager awakening shrugged and lifted his hands. He knew the lock Miss Gipson had insisted on having installed was inferior to the standard locks on the other apartment doors in the building. He had told her so; the man who installed the lock had told her so. But she had insisted; she had thought they were trying to talk her out of their trouble and expense. She had said it was non-sense to expect her to trust to a lock like hundreds of others, all openable with a master key.

"How about the maid?" Weigand asked.

"Naturally," the manager said, "she had to have a key. Even Miss Gipson admitted that. But the key had to be kept at the desk—the girl had to get it each time she did the room and return it after she had finished. Miss Gipson checked up periodically."

"And the key was always to be accounted for?" Weigand asked.

The manager smiled faintly. He said there had been a couple of times; he said Miss Gipson wanted them to fire the maid. He pointed out that it would have been much easier to replace Miss Gipson; there was a suggestion that he had, tactfully, conveyed this fact of post-war housing to her. He wanted to know, in that connection, when the apartment would be available for a new tenant.

"We'll get enquiries tomorrow, you know," he said. "When this hits the newspapers. If her address is given. People are"—he paused, picking words—"quite anxious for apartments."

Weigand said it might be a week or so and the manager looked disappointed. He said that the whole thing was a great inconvenience.

Bill Weigand admitted that it probably was; he joined the Norths, waiting by the door, and interrupted their conversation with the doorman.

"He says she went out about six," Pam told him. "He supposed to dinner."

Bill said he supposed the same thing.

Pam wanted to know where now? The Library, Bill told her, to see how things went there.

"Then?" Pam said.

Then, Bill Weigand thought, his office and home, until morning.

"Not my office?" Jerry said.

That would keep, Bill thought. It would keep until tomorrow.

"She might have notes there," Pam said.

Bill agreed she might. He said the notes would keep. He asked if they wanted a lift home in the police car. Jerry North was ready to say yes, but he found that Pam was shaking her head at him.

"We'll walk," Pam said. "It's only a few blocks. Won't we, Jerry? And such a nice night."

Jerry agreed they would walk.

Gerald North paid off the taxi driver and looked without pleasure at the elderly office building on Fourth Avenue in the low Thirties. He looked at his watch and said that, of course, it was almost two o'clock.

"In the morning," he added.

"It won't," Pam told him, "take a minute. We'll just get her notes before somebody else does and see if there's anything else. That somebody might want. I think Bill should have, but after all it's your office."

After all, Jerry said, he had spent the day in it. He would spend tomorrow in it.

"Today," he said, morosely. "Beginning in seven hours."

But they had crossed the sidewalk to the building entrance and opened the door. It was a building in which publishers nested, gregariously. It was a building to which some of them, sometimes, came late at night, usually to get things they had forgotten. So, although the building belonged to an era when doors were locked at night, its door was not locked. An elderly man slept uneasily on guard by the two elevators. Jerry signed the night register and looked at the guard.

"Poor thing," Pam said. "We could walk."

Sympathy, Jerry told her, began at home. They could ride. The guard awoke unwillingly and looked at the Norths without enthusiasm. He said "God," with the resignation of one who has ceased to expect an answer. He looked at the stairway which ran up beside the elevators and his look was reproachful. He got up and went to the elevator and into it without saying anything, and waited. When the Norths got in he took them up. He stopped at the fifth floor and they got out. He followed them for a step or two and when they looked at him he looked fixedly at the staircase. Then he got into the elevator and disappeared with it.

"We'll walk down," Pam said. "The poor man."

Jerry said nothing but went along the hall until he came to a door at the end marked "North Books, Inc." He opened the door with his key and stopped and looked at his key.

"Listen," he said. "Where was her key? Miss Gipson's? To this door; to her own door at home. To whatever else she had a right to open? Were they in her bag?"

Pam shook her head. She said the police had probably taken them out.

"Bill got the maid's key from the manager," Jerry told her. "To the apartment. He didn't have it."

Pam said it was odd, without seeming to think it

odd, and why didn't they go in? They went in. Jerry switched on the lights in the reception-room, comfortable in modern furniture. It was a wide, shallow room, with doors at either end and near the ends in the wall opposite the entrance door. Jerry went to the door in the opposite wall at the right end and threw another tumbler switch, lighting the offices. He went down an inner corridor, with a railing on one side and beyond it desks with typewriters hibernating in them. He switched on more lights in a small office at the end of the corridor. He waved at it and sat down in a chair.

"Miss Gipson's," he said. "Her copies of her notes are in the lower right-hand drawer of the desk. Each copy is clipped to the notebook in which she made her original notes. She used one notebook for each case. My copies are in my office. The originals have been sent to the authors who are going to use them." He sighed and appeared to go to sleep. He roused himself. "It's all yours," he said. "Wake me up when we get home."

Pam North looked in the lower right-hand drawer of the desk. Then she looked at Jerry.

"I'm sorry, Jerry," she said, "but you did say 'right?' Because they aren't, you know."

"They were," he said. "I suppose she moved them. Look, darling."

Pam looked. Then she looked at Jerry.

"Listen, Jerry," she said. "Are you sure this is the right office? Because there's nothing in the desk. Nothing at all." She paused. "Except some old paper clips and things, of course," she said. "No notes. No letters."

"I tell you—" Jerry said, and suddenly sat up. He went to the desk and pulled out the drawers one after another and shut them again. He looked at Pam. He was no longer sleepy.

"We were late," Pam said. "In spite of everything, we were late."

"Jerry nodded. He said there had evidently been something in Miss Gipson's desk that somebody wanted.

"Her murderer," Pam said.

"You jump, Pam," Jerry said. "But probably her murderer."

"You wouldn't like me if I didn't jump," Pam said. "We both know that. And it's foolish to call it a jump. He wanted her notes on the famous crimes."

Jerry shook his head at that. He pointed out that that really was a jump. He said it might have been anything—anything that collects in an office desk, even in a month. Letters received at the office, or carried to the office for rereading and left in the desk. Little memoranda, scrawled on slips of paper. Or written on desk calendars.

They had both thought of that at the same moment. Their heads met over the desk. The desk calendar was there. The uppermost sheet said Tuesday, September 11. But the old sheets—the turned-back sheets—were missing. Two-thirds of the year had vanished. And the past month of Amelia Gipson's life.

"Well," Pam said.

She watched as Jerry leafed into the future, which was not to be Miss Gipson's future. In early October there was one notation: "Dentist, 2 P.M." That was to have been on October 9. Beyond that, in so far as she had confided to her desk calendar, Miss Gipson had had no plans.

"Perhaps she tore the old ones off and threw them away after they were finished," Pam said. "The old days."

"Perhaps," Jerry said. "But I never knew anyone who did, did you? From this kind of a calendar, with rings meant to—to hold the past? For reference? Because that's one thing calendars on office desks are for. Day before yesterday's telephone numbers— things like that."

Pam was nodding slowly.

"What happened," she said, "was that everything was taken. Whether it meant anything or not. So we wouldn't know what *did* mean something. Don't you suppose it was that way?"

Jerry agreed it could have been. He was looking

thoughtfully at nothing. Then he said, "Wait here a minute, Pam," and went out of the office, and she could hear his steps going down the corridor. She stopped hearing them and waited in an office which had grown very still. She waited until surely it was time for him to come back. And then the lights in the general office went out. Pam was on her feet and crying, "Jerry! Jerry!" with her voice rising and then she was running through the office, dim and shadowy with only the light from the office behind her to dispel the darkness. As she ran toward Jerry's office she saw that there was no light in it.

She was not afraid, except for Jerry. She forgot to be afraid. But it took her a moment to find the tumbler switch inside the door of Jerry's office. And then she screamed, because Jerry North was on his hands and knees on the floor and was shaking his head in a puzzled fashion. She ran to him, but by then he was getting up and she stopped. There was a bruise on his forehead and in the center of it a thin line of blood where the skin was broken.

"Jerry!" she said. *"Darling!* Oh darling! Are you—"

She stopped, because, although his face was puzzled and not quite all together, Jerry was grinning at her.

"No, Pam," he said, "I'm not all right, as you see. But I'm all right. I just bumped my head."

"Somebody hit you!" Pam said. Her voice was high and tense.

Jerry started to shake his head and then stopped shaking it and put a hand to it. He saw blood on his hand and began to dab at the blood with a handkerchief.

"I fell into the desk," he said. "Nobody hit me. But somebody pushed me. From behind, hard. Just as I was reaching for the light switch. It—it caught me off balance. And so I fell into the desk. It—it dazed me for a minute. But I'm all right."

"Darling!" Pam said. "And I got you into it. You didn't want to come. I made you."

Jerry said it was all right.

"Come on," Pam said. "We'll go right home. We'll get a doctor. We'll—"

But Jerry, a little unsteadily, was opening a drawer in his desk. He brought out a handful of typewritten sheets.

"Miss Gipson's notes," he said. "On the four cases she'd finished. My copies. So they weren't—"

He stopped, because Pam did not seem to be listening to him.

"Jerry!" Pam said. "There's perfume in here. There was in Miss Gipson's office, too, but I was too excited to realize it. The same perfume."

Jerry tested the air. He nodded.

"Not mine," Pam said. "Not what I'm wearing now, as it wasn't before. That Fleur de Something or Other. The same as was in her apartment. The murderer's perfume."

Jerry did not say, this time, that she was jumping. He said he thought they ought to get out of there. They went out, leaving the lights burning behind them. It was Pam who rang the elevator bell, and kept on ringing it until the building guard brought the elevator up and glowered at them. This time he spoke, but not until they were at the ground floor.

"People could use the stairs," he said then. "Coming down, anyway. Other people do."

"Who does?" Pam said, quickly.

"Whoever just went out, of course," he said. Who did you think?"

"But who was it?" Pam said.

He shook his head at that.

"I just heard them," he said. "I didn't see nobody. Just steps woke me up, but they were gone before I looked."

4

The grist was coming in. Bill Weigand, drinking coffee out of a paper container and abstractedly eating an egg sandwich, looked at it without enthusiasm. One hundred and thirty-three men and women, and boys and girls, had filed slips at the central desk in the main reference room between seven o'clock the evening before and closing time. The slips included, along with titles and catalogue numbers, the names and addresses of the readers. Few of these were particularly legible; there was no reason to suppose that, if the murderer were one of them, the murderer would have signed a name and given an address. He—to use a pronoun which was probably erroneous in gender—need not have turned in a slip at all. That was not required; certainly in his case it would not have been indicated. He could have walked through the catalogue room and into either the North or South Reading Rooms and no one would have questioned him. He could have been looking a word up in a dictionary. He could have been reading the Britannica. Or he could merely have been looking for Miss Amelia Gipson, to see how the poison was working on her.

That he had been here seemed probable. It had not seemed probable, because obviously it was not necessary for his plan, until Gerald North had called at 2:30 that morning and told of the ransacking of Miss Gip-

son's desk at North Books, Inc.; told also of having
been pushed into his own desk; added aggrievedly that
he had a headache as a result. The intruder had had
keys to the office, Jerry North pointed out. Presumably they were Miss Gipson's keys. Didn't Bill
think?

Bill Weigand did think. And in that event, the
chances were high that—unless, of course, Miss Gipson had given her murderer the keys to the North
offices, to facilitate his heavy task—the keys had been
taken from the Gipson purse in the confusion which
followed her violent attack of illness in the North
Reading Room of the Library. Therefore, the murderer was in the North Reading Room of the Library.
The murderer had not taken the folding drinking cup
from the purse. Therefore, the murderer had not
minded their discovering that a concentrated solution
of sodium fluoride had been drunk from the cup. That
was not puzzling. Presence of the cup, with its traces
of poison, would encourage them to think of suicide.
Only Miss Gipson had got the better of her murderer
there.

Bill Weigand sighed, reached for the remains of his
sandwich and found there were no remains. He finished his paper cup of coffee, savoring the taste of
cardboard—the slight fuzziness of texture which probably was attributable to dissolved wood pulp—and
sighed. He was reminded of Deputy Chief Inspector
Artemus O'Malley.

O'Malley still believed in suicide. He thought the
last line Miss Gipson had written, in a hand firm up to
the end—before it was no longer a living hand, but a
dying one in which a fountain pen trailed
meaninglessly—was merely something she had written
about the Purdy case. She was taking notes on a
poison murder, wasn't she? The last line mentioned
poison, didn't it? Well?

"The trouble with you, Weigand," O'Malley said at
2:35 that morning, just after the Norths had called and
just as he was going home to bed—"the trouble with
you, Weigand, is that you let the Norths ball things up.

Here you've got a nice simple suicide and you let the Norths ball you up. Snafu!"

The word *snafu* had come late into Inspector O'Malley's life. He liked it, although sometimes Weigand wondered whether he exactly understood it. It had come to mean anything unduly complicated; anything out of the classic tradition of police work. "Round 'em up and make 'em talk's what I always say," O'Malley always did say. Bill Weigand could only think that, in O'Malley's more active days, crime had had a pleasing simplicity which now it lacked. He sighed again and dropped the container which had held coffee—perhaps—into a wastebasket. He drummed lightly with the fingers of his right hand on the desk top.

One hundred and thirty-three men and women, boys and girls, to be interviewed, to see whether they knew anything; had seen anything. Say a dozen of them had given false addresses; in New York it was safe, he thought, that twelve out of a hundred and thirty-three would give false names and addresses for reasons of their own—reasons absurd and serious, obvious and obscure and having, the chances went a hundred to one, no connection whatever with the demise of Miss Amelia Gipson, fifty-two years old, lately of Ward College, more lately of North Books, Inc., having a niece who did not care for her and a friend who was frightened, and no need to take a forty-dollar-a-week job for which she had no special training and probably no consuming interest.

One hundred and thirty-three of all ages and both sexes, a dozen of whom would be troublesome to find and must, even more than the rest, be found. Because it was never certain that their desire for anonymity had not grown out of the murder of Miss Amelia Gipson. Such a search for privacy, if excessive, was not criminal. Still—it was odd; still it needed explanation. The solution of crime almost inevitably involved the clearing of a half-dozen irrelevant mysteries, few of which any longer interested Bill Weigand. Particularly at 7:30 in the morning, after a night of work; particularly when Dorian was out of town and had taken her smile, so curiously refreshing, with her and would not be back for another six full days, plus an entirely uncalled for six hours.

The hundred and thirty-three could be left to the precincts, as could the majority of the attendants on duty when Miss Gipson had been taken ill. That was something; all Weigand and his own people would have to do would be to collate the information, if any was gathered. It would be pleasant if one of the hundred and thirty-three had seen Miss Gipson in the grip of a powerful man with a black beard, one leg and other arresting peculiarities and had seen this spectacular creature pouring poison forcefully into her mouth. Bill Weigand was afraid that so simple a pleasure would be denied him. He thought the attendant, already questioned, who had seen Miss Gipson pass through the catalogue room into the outer hall and return a little later, and who had deduced that she had gone down the hall to drink from one of the wall fountains, had told them as much as anybody would be apt to about the actual injection of the poison.

But someone, among those who had gathered around Miss Gipson when she suddenly made a terrible sound, which was half scream and half retching, and collapsed sideways over the arm of the chair, might have seen something of significance. One of them might have seen a man—or, if perfume meant anything, a woman—handling Miss Gipson's purse; might even have seen someone take something out of it. That would be very helpful. Unfortunately, only three of those persons had lingered long enough to be interrogated by the patrolman who first reached the scene. Weigand read over the terse reports of their interrogation:

"Roger Burnside, student, of 201A Grand Concourse, the Bronx, said he was sitting across from deceased and had his attention attracted by a strange sound emanating from her. Describes sound as a low scream. Looked up to see her staring at him. He thinks she tried to speak and could not. He thinks she was writing something. Says she then collapsed across arm of chair in which she was sitting and began to vomit. Went to her assistance but was preceded by several other persons, none of whom he can describe, and found his assistance unnecessary. Remained on the chance it might be."

"Florence Pettley, housewife: Was looking up recipes in a cookbook when heard strange, dreadful sound behind her and turned around to find elderly woman apparently very ill. Asked to describe illness, said: 'She seemed to be sick at her stomach.' Went to her and found her moaning and apparently unable to speak; very sick at the stomach. Held deceased's head and tried to talk to her, but doubts if deceased heard or understood."

"John Gallahady, unemployed, was reading old copies of *The New Yorker* at table on other side of central aisle: Heard retching sound from elderly woman who looked like a teacher in a fresh-water college and saw her begin to throw up. Went to see what he could do to help and decided there was nothing, but remained on chance there might be. Started to leave when he himself became nauseated but was stopped by arrival of police, who asked him to remain, since he had been a witness. Remembers plump housewife—presumably a reference to Mrs. Pettley—fussing about but did not particularly notice anyone else."

Those were the ones they had. There were then only one hundred and thirty to go. The others probably would be even less helpful. Then, just as he was about to toss the three reports into a basket, he paused. About one of the interviews there had been something that lingered, faintly disturbing, in his memory. He looked at them again.

The last person—John Gallahady—had been a good guesser. Ward College would not like being called "fresh-water." But it was a small college and not famous. Mr. Gallahady was acute. It might be interesting to know what made him so acute. Weigand rummaged among the papers on his desk and found the

typed, alphabetized, list of persons who had signed out
for books. He ran a pencil down the *G's*. No Gallahady. No—

"Damn," Weigand said. "Of course!"

There were only eleven now to be discovered among
those who had used false names. One was found. For
Gallahady, read Galahad. Caxton, setting up the type
for Sir Thomas Malory's "Noble and Joyous Book
entytled Le Morte d'Arthur" had once reversed that
reading, for Galahad had set Gallahady. Weigand
groped to ascertain how he knew this. Then, dimly, he
remembered that he had been reading the Noble Tale
in a reprint edition on a rainy day in the country during
the summer; reading it lacking all other reading. And
had seen a footnote and remembered it.

So John Gallahady was Sir Galahad, going to the
succor of a distressed gentlewoman, was he? Very
fanciful, the unemployed gentleman who had been
reading *The New Yorker* in the Library and had not
quite got away before the police came. A little pedantic in his allusions. Weigand thought it would be interesting to talk to Mr. Gallahady and wished he could.
The chances did not seem good; false name probably
meant also false address—an address in the West
Fifties. Bill Weigand looked at the address, which
somehow seemed authentic. A good many unemployed gentlemen lived in those blocks, in small, dusty
rooms. There was a chance that Gallahady, having
little time to think, had given an authentic address—
addresses were harder to think of than names, sometimes, particularly if you did not very well know the
city.

Weigand got the West Forty-eighth Street police
station on the telephone. The precinct would be glad to
send a man around. If they found Gallahady they
would bring him in.

"Irish, sounds like," O'Callahan, on the desk, told
Bill Weigand. "Irish, is he?"

"He could be," Bill said. He smiled slightly to
himself. "I've sometimes thought he must have been,"

Weigand said. "An extremist, it always seemed to me."

"Huh?" O'Callahan said.

Weigand told him to skip it. Weigand said he had been talking to himself. He replaced the telephone, looked at it and heard it ring. He took it up and said, "Homicide. Weigand speaking."

"Hello, loot," Mullins said. "Look, loot. I'm up here at the girl's room. The girl who cleaned up Miss Gipson's room."

"The room of the girl who cleaned up Miss Gipson's room," Bill Weigand said. "The pen of my aunt."

"What?" Mullins said. "I don't get it, loot."

"I know where you are," Bill said. "I told you to go there. What does she say?"

"Nothing," Mullins said. "She ain't here."

"Why?" Weigand said. "I thought she wasn't due at the hotel until ten. She's probably out to breakfast."

"I got here at seven," Mullins said. "She wasn't here then. She wasn't here last night, from the looks of things. The bed, you know, loot."

Weigand said he knew.

"And," Mullins said, "her clothes ain't here, either. Anyway, not enough clothes. Of course, maybe she didn't have many clothes."

"Listen," Bill said. "You mean she's skipped?"

Wasn't that, Mullins said, what he was telling the loot? It looked like she had skipped.

"Or of course," Mullins added, in a conversational tone, "somebody could have bumped her off. Naturally."

"Right," Weigand said. He looked at his desk, and was displeased by it. Outside it looked like a pleasant morning.

"Hold it," Weigand told Mullins. "I'm coming up."

Florence Adams, who had been a maid at the Holborn Annex, had lived in a rooming house a few blocks from Columbia University—lived in a small

room which looked unlived in. There was a worn black
coat hanging in the tiny, low closet which opened off
the room; on the cheap dresser there were traces of
powder and in the wastebasket there were several
wads of used cleansing tissue. Weigand sniffed at the
cleansing tissue, which smelled of cold cream; he
sniffed the coat, which smelled of dust. There was
nothing in the room which smelled of the Fleur de
Something or Other which had been so quietly insistent in Miss Gipson's room. And there was nothing in
the room to tell him anything about Florence Adams,
or to tell him where she had gone.

There was, Mullins agreed, nothing to suggest that
she had met with ill fortune, including the very ill
fortune of being bumped off.

"Only," Mullins said, "people are. We ought to
know that, loot. Particularly when they lend keys to
murderers to have copies made. It ain't healthy."
Mullins paused. "Or, of course," he said, "she could
be the one we're looking for. There's always that,
too."

There was, Weigand agreed. Certainly she was one
of the ones they were looking for now. His eyes kept
searching the room, looking for secrets in it. He knelt
and looked under the bed, and saw only dust. He
turned back the covers. The sheets had been used for a
week, he guessed; perhaps for two weeks. Near the
bed there was a shelf which might have contained
books and which now contained nothing. As far as he
could see, the room—possibly with a change of
sheets—was ready for the next tenant who passed that
way.

It was odd, he thought suddenly, how easy it was to
overlook the obvious. Yesterday's newspaper was not
only dead; apparently it was invisible. Or had been
invisible. Now it was visible enough, lying on the seat
of the straight chair by the dusty window. He picked it
up. It was *The Daily News* of that morning, turned
open at the second page. There was a very short story
there—a paragraph inserted for the record. The top
line of the head read: "Poisoned in Library." The bank

amplified: "Middle-aged Woman dies in Reading Room." The story added little to the headline, except the possibility that the woman may have been an Amelia Gibson, living at the Bolborn Annex and that her death apparently was suicide.

A police slip at Headquarters had given them that much to make an edition with—to make it on the outside chance that it might not be suicide, because poison in the Public Library had the charm of novelty. The story had been written, evidently, before an astute detective, making a routine check of a suspicious death, had come upon the last line which Miss Gipson had written and decided it might be a case for Homicide. Later editions of *The News* had had more. The story had flowered, not only in *The News* but in *The Mirror*. It had made the split page in *The Herald Tribune* and had got a two-column head, below the fold, of course, in *The Times*. It would be doing a great deal better in the afternoons, Weigand thought.

Florence Adams had not waited its flowering. She had seen enough in the edition of *The News* on street sale by midnight to satisfy her curiosity. You could read that much easily; Weigand hoped he read it rightly. Because if he did, Florence Adams knew something—had done something—which led her into flight. It was always helpful when people began to run. It was revealing. And they were almost always caught.

Bill Weigand found a telephone and talked to the Holborn Annex. Florence Adams was not there; she was not due there for better than an hour.

"By the way," the desk clerk said, "one of your men is here, lieutenant. Detective O'Connor? He's been talking to one of the other maids—the one on the early trick. Do you want to talk to him?"

Weigand thought he did. He listened to O'Connor, said "Right," and hung up.

"O'Connor says the other girl—a woman of about sixty, by the way—says Florence never used any perfume that she could smell," Weigand told Mullins. "And he got a description of Florence for us."

Twenty minutes later the description was on the

teletype. It went into police stations throughout New York and New Jersey; it went into Connecticut and across into Pennsylvania; it stuttered out of machines in Massachusetts.

"Wanted for questioning," it said. "Florence Adams; about 24, black hair, sallow complexion; about 115 pounds; five feet three; may have been wearing brown wool two-piece dress, beige stockings, black shoes. Sometimes wears glasses with white metal rims. Believed myopic. No coloring on fingernails. Identifiable New York City accent. This woman is wanted for questioning in connection Gipson murder. Please hold."

By the time an operator at Headquarters was fingering the description out on the teletype, Weigand and Mullins were back in Weigand's office. And they were waiting for Mr. Gallahady, who had been sitting placidly in his room in the West Fifties, reading *PM*. He had not seemed surprised when a detective from the precinct said that there were one or two points they would like cleared up, and would he mind being run downtown to offices of detectives in charge of the case. Gallahady had said he did not mind in the least; he had been very cheerful about it. He had also agreed that his name was Philip Spencer, confirming the statement of his landlady.

Bill Weigand did not wait long. They brought Gallahady-Spencer in to him and, invited, Gallahady-Spencer sat down. Mullins, at a nod from Weigand, got a notebook ready.

"By the way," Weigand said, "why Gallahady?"

The man who sat, easily and with apparent confidence, was in his middle forties. He needed a shave and a haircut; he needed a new suit and new shoes; he needed, Weigand thought suddenly, a new life. There was a laxness about his face; a kind of hopeless softness and he smelled a little as if he had been drinking a good deal for a long time.

But nothing in his manner apologized for any of this; nothing in his manner admitted any of this. If he had fought it once, he was no longer fighting it.

"A jest," he said, answering Bill Weigand's question. "Possibly pedantic. I borrowed it from—"

Bill's nod stopped him. Bill said he knew where the name had been borrowed from. He perceived the jest. Spencer raised his eyebrows as he listened; he seemed surprised.

"Aside from Caxton's little error," Weigand said, "why any false name? Why not your own name, Mr. Spencer?"

Spencer said it was a whim. He said he didn't know why. He pointed out that he had, in any event, given his correct address.

"Probably," Bill told him, "because it is difficult to think of a convincing address in a city you don't know very well—when you are talking to men who know it very well." And Spencer could skip the whim part of it.

"Do you know, lieutenant, I think you may be quite right about the address business," Spencer said. He spoke with a kind of detached interest. "I wondered why I didn't give a fictitious address. I think you have explained it."

Bill held him to it. It wasn't a whim, he pointed out again. He pointed out, also, that they were investigating a case of murder.

"Why," Bill said, "did you go to the trouble to hide your identity, Mr. Spencer? Has your identity something to do with the case?

Spencer hesitated, clearly making up his mind what to say. Then he said that Weigand might think his identity had something to do with the case.

"I knew Amelia," he said. "Naturally, I say I had nothing to do with her taking off. But you would expect me to say that."

"Right," Bill Weigand said. He waited.

"It was a very unfortunate coincidence, for me," Spencer said. "Very unfortunate. I might have been almost any other place. I might have been in South Reading Room instead of North Reading Room. It would have made no difference to Amelia, believe me. But oh, the difference to me."

Weigand waited.

"I wish you would believe it was entirely a coincidence," Spencer said. He spoke almost wistfully.

Still Weigand said nothing. Spencer looked at the detective lieutenant's face and then he shrugged. They might as well have it, he told them, and waited until Mullins was ready.

"Name," he said. "Philip Spencer. With one 'l.' Philip Spencer, Ph.D. Age, 43. Occupation, former associate professor of English at Ward College, Rushton, Indiana. Dismissed for unbecoming conduct with one of the students—one of the girls. Because a spiteful little fool told a lot of lies to a spiteful old bitch who—" He broke off. He smiled, and the smile was contorted. He began again.

"Too much coincidence," he said. "Even for me. And yet it's true. The girl, who I swear misunderstood something which was entirely innocent, went to Miss Amelia Gipson—Gipson with a *p*, mind you—who was head of the Latin Department and also a sort of unofficial censor of morals. And Amelia went to the president of the school, who was a friend of mine but not—well, not that good a friend. Understandable—the school was all he had. It had to be above suspicion. Well—I wasn't. So he had to let me go. He was as quiet about it as he could be—as decent. But Amelia saw the word got around."

He paused and looked off at nothing.

"Schools are touchy," he said. "Big schools and little schools. Faculty members of girls' colleges who are suspected of—molesting—their charges don't find it easy to get jobs. And teachers in their forties—just good enough teachers—don't find it easy to get other jobs."

He looked at Mullins. He asked Mullins if he was getting it all. Mullins said "yeah."

"I was married," he said. "My wife was not in good health. Possibly that is one of the reasons I had remained at Ward; because of the security. My wife died about six months after I—left the faculty. Our living conditions weren't what they had been and, as I said, she was not in good health. I have been somewhat—somewhat detached from life ever since. I had even almost forgotten Amelia until I saw her at the Library last night. You will hardly believe that, but it's true. I heard she has also left the faculty. It seems there were—other cases. Rather like mine, except that in the end she seems to have been imagining them. She made one or two mistakes—imagined one or two impossibilities, I suppose—and the head suggested that she leave."

Spencer was silent for a moment, regarding the past as if it were in the room.

"There was a suggestion that I might return to Ward after Amelia left," he said, at length, quietly. "It seemed rather late. Rather too late."

He stopped speaking again and this time he did not resume. Weigand waited and after a time asked whether that was all of it.

"That's all of it," Spencer said. "I was there. You could make a motive out of what I've told you. There isn't anything else. I can't prove I didn't give her whatever she died of. I don't even know what it was. I didn't see anything suspicious, so I can't put you on a trail."

This time it was Weigand who established the silence and let it lie in the office. And it was Spencer who suddenly leaned forward in his chair.

"Well, lieutenant?" he said.

Bill Weigand looked at him, with no particular expression, and shook his head.

"It's not that easy, Mr. Spencer," he said. "You can see that. You know what the truth is, so far as you are concerned. You have the advantage of me. I don't know. All I know is what you say."

"Which," Spencer said, "you see no reason to believe."

It was not a question. But Bill Weigand said it was not even that easy.

"Which," he said, "I have no grounds to form an opinion on. At the moment, it is equally possible you are telling the truth and lying. There is nothing impos-

sible in your story, as you know. Since you are not, so
far as I can see, a fool, there wouldn't be anything
impossible in the story. I'll have to look into it."

"And let me know," Spencer finished.

He need have no doubt of that, Weigand promised
him, and there was a certain grimness in his promise.
Meanwhile, Mr. Spencer would—

"Hold myself available," Spencer finished. "Or do
you hold me available?"

Weigand smiled pleasantly, and told him the former,
by all means.

"Of course," he said, "we might take a hand if it
became necessary. I assume it won't. I assume we'll
be able to find you at your room when we want you."

Spencer stood up. Weigand looked up at him, saying
nothing. Spencer hesitated a moment, as if he were
about to say more, and then said, "Well, all right" in
an uncertain fashion, and then, "Goodbye."

"Goodbye, Mr. Spencer," Weigand said, politely.
"Probably I'll be seeing you."

Spencer did not look happy. He went. Mullins,
looking after him, shook his head.

"O'Malley," Mullins said, "ain't going to like it,
loot. Next best to suicide, this guy Spencer is. Opportunity, motive, present on the scene, false name—hell,
he's made for it."

Bill said he gathered Mullins wasn't buying Spencer's story. Mullins shrugged. He said it wasn't him, it
was the inspector. He looked at Weigand.

"How about you, loot?" he said.

Weigand's fingers were drumming gently on his
desk. He did not look up. For a moment he did not
speak. Then he said he didn't like coincidences.

"It needs a lot of believing, Spencer's story," he
said. "But, as I told him, it's possible. And we can't
hang him on it. O'Malley couldn't, I couldn't. The
commissioner couldn't or the D.A., so we waits and
sees."

Again Mullins waited. He saw Weigand look at the
watch on his wrist, and then up at the clock on the
wall. Weigand said they ought to be hearing from

Stein. Mullins looked enquiring. Weigand said Stein was at the lawyer's office.

"Williams, Franke and something or other," he said. "Miss Gipson's attorneys. Attorneys for the estate she was handling. The people who know—"

The telephone on his desk rang and he spoke into it. He said, "All right, Stein, come along up." He replaced the receiver and said, "Speaking of coincidences."

They waited, looking at the door, and Detective Sergeant Stein came in. He was a trim, slender man in his thirties, with dark, absorbed eyes. He sat down where Spencer had sat. He said he had seen a man named Mason. He said Mason had given him the dope.

Amelia Gipson was the daughter of Alfred Gipson, Stein said, checking with his notes as he talked. Alfred Gipson had died, leaving a good deal of money, in 1901. He had left it to his wife in trust and, on her death two years later, it had been divided between the two children, Amelia and Alfred Gipson, Jr. Each had received around three hundred thousand dollars. Amelia had put hers, for the most part, in bonds; a good deal of it in government bonds. She had lived on the interest; until recently, when taxes went up and interest down, she had done a little better than live on the interest. But say she left about the same sum she had inherited.

"To?" Weigand said.

Stein said he was coming to that. He said it wasn't, he thought, the most important thing. But she had left the bulk of it to a nephew and a niece, in equal shares. To get back, he said.

Alfred, Jr., Amelia's brother, had been about ten years older than Amelia—he had been born in 1883, and had been twenty when his mother died. And at twenty, apparently, he had started making money. He had made it, sometimes rapidly, sometimes slowly, but almost always consistently, until he died in 1940. He had also found time to marry and beget two children. His wife died when her daughter was born in 1922, which made the daughter twenty-three. The son was

two years older. That was John. The girl was Nora.
But no longer Nora Gipson. Now Nora Frost, wife of
Major Kennet Frost.

"Air Force major," Stein said. "He's been in the
Pacific. But he got back Stateside yesterday, Mason
thinks. They expect him in New York today some
time. Everybody's all steamed up—or everybody was
yesterday. The aunt's death—made a difference, Mason supposes, to get back."

Alfred Gipson, who had dropped the junior when his
father died, had brought up the children with some
advice from his sister, who, however, had apparently
exercised a rather distant supervision, except in the
summers, when she had joined the family at a place
they had in Maine. She and the children, with enough
servants, had spent most summers there when John
and Nora were growing up, and Alfred had come up
for long weekends and sometimes for a week or two at
a time.

Alfred Gipson had had almost a year's warning of
his death. He had drawn up his will when John was
nineteen and Nora seventeen. He left his money—
which ran to about a million and a half after taxes—to
his sister in trust for the children, with the proviso that
it was to be divided between them when Nora was
twenty-five. Stein paused and looked up.

"Or," he said, "upon the death of Amelia Gipson,
whichever should occur first."

Weigand nodded slowly.

"So the children cut up a million and a half," he
said. "Plus Amelia's share."

"Less tax," Stein said.

"Less tax," Bill Weigand agreed. "Still all right, I
should think. The next question—are the children hard
up?"

Mason said not, Stein told him. Major Frost had
some money—not the same kind of money, but some.

"And John's probably in the Army," Weigand said.
"Or the Navy?"

Stein shook his head.

"Apparently not," he said. "John's a chemist—for

his age, Mason things a pretty important chemist. Too important to get killed, unless he blows himself up. Mason seemed to think there was a pretty good chance he would, although the stuff he's working on is all very secret. Has been right along. Mason thinks now it may have had something to do with the atomic bombs, but he still doesn't know. And John's still working at it. Up in Connecticut somewhere, apparently a good way from other people except the people he's working with. Only he's in town now."

"Why?" Weigand wanted to know.

Stein shrugged. He said he had asked Mason. He said Mason didn't know.

"Mason says if anybody knows, it's Backley," Stein said. "Backley is another member of the firm. He's out of town, but's expected back this evening. Mason says Backley is the man who has really handled the Gipson affairs and had most of the personal contacts with them. He says we'll want to talk to Backley."

Weigand nodded. He said they would.

"And," he said, "with the children," He tapped his desk gently. "Rather soon," he added.

5

Amelia Gipson had completed research into three murder cases before she provided one. The results lay on Pamela North's desk in neat typescript. They were summaries; the skeletons of old tragedies. The one uppermost was headed: "Notes on the Joyce Wentworth Murder for Mr. Hill." Mr. Hill was the writer who would put the intangible flesh of words on the skeleton of fact Miss Gipson had provided. It was cut to Mr. Hill's taste, was the Wentworth murder. It was unsolved and meaningless; it piqued the curiosity which it so little satisfied. It would give Mr. Hill room to turn around in, which was what Mr. Hill liked. His own series, "Fancies in Death," presented—some suggested more than anything else—the spectacle of Mr. Hill turning around. The whimsically macabre was Mr. Hill's dish.

With the Wentworth case, Pam North decided, Mr. Hill could do practically anything—hint at things most strange and wonderful. Nobody was ever going to call him to account, setting cold fact against his artful imagining. There was very little cold fact.

The coal of Pam's cigarette, which was held in the hand against which she rested her cheek as she read, nestled in her hair. There was a faint, acrid scent of burning hair. Pam sniffed, said "Oh, not *again*" aloud to herself and brushed at her hair violently. She got up and looked at it in a mirror and said, without surprise, "Damn." She went back to the script.

Nobody knew who had killed Joyce Wentworth, or why she had been killed. It was likely, unless Mr. Hill could dream up a solution, that nobody would ever know either of these facts. Joyce Wentworth had been a tall, slender girl with a thin, sculptured face and pale red hair. She had earned her living by wearing clothes which looked on her as they would never look on anyone else—by walking, with a faint and detached smile on her really lovely face, through the aisles of one of the big Fifth Avenue stores. Sometimes, although it might be eleven in the morning, she wore evening dress; sometimes, although it might be August, she wore furs; often she wore suits and street dresses, but always it was possible to tell that she was not merely a customer, but a dream provided by the management. Women who had rather more than Joyce Wentworth's figure, although not always so judiciously arranged, sometimes identified themselves with the dream and purchased the evening dresses, the furs, the coats and suits and street dresses, which she made resplendent. And often they wondered, afterward, what it was that had gone wrong between dream and realization.

Joyce Wentworth had been wearing her own clothes, which were merely clothes and not creations, when she had been killed. She had been walking from the bus stop nearest her home in the Murray Hill section—a one-room-and-bath home, quite in proportion to her salary—and it had been not quite dark on a winter's afternoon. It was assumed she was walking home; she had been talking to one of the salesgirls at the store on the bus, and had said she was going home.

That was in 1942—December 11, 1942—and the streets were partly lighted but not light enough. Apparently somebody had hidden in the shadow of a building entrance, let the girl pass and then stepped up behind her and stuck a kitchen knife in her back. Whoever it was had left the knife there and walked away. The girl had managed to walk almost a quarter of a block before she fell. She was still alive when she was found, about ten minutes later. She had died in an ambulance and had never said anything to anyone.

It was, as one newspaper writer had pointed out, a perfect murder. Miss Gipson had quoted a sentence or two from the newspaper story in her notes. "This," the newspaper specialist in crime had written, "is the way to commit murder if you want to murder. This crime has classic simplicity. Overtake your victim on a quiet street, stab or bludgeon or throttle, walk away. Complication may trap you—leave booby traps, intricate time tables, alibis—to the writers of mysteries. Waylay, strike and walk away. The chance is good that you will be safe. If you have no motive, you are almost certain to be safe."

The murderer of Joyce Wentworth, at any rate, had been safe. He was safe today. He had dropped nothing; he had left no fingerprints. There was nothing the police could find in the girl's past to give motive for her death. The police had hinted at a jealous lover; they could produce no lover, jealous or satisfied. They had sought a triangle, but Joyce Wentworth's life had been, so far as they could discover, a straight line—a line leading from a small town in Indiana to death in East Thirty-sixth Street.

The very simplicity of the case—its starkness—had, coupled with the girl's quite striking beauty, given the murder celebrity. A great deal had been written about it in 1942; it had since then become a reference point in all surveys of murder in America. Now Mr. Hill was to do it for, presumably, all time.

"With curlicues," Pam North said to herself.

She laid the typescript face down and thought it over. That was the task she had set herself. She had told Jerry so at breakfast, which was rather later than usual; she had said that Bill was obviously going to work with Miss Gipson's family, because he assumed the solution of her murder lay in that direction. Or with Helen Burt, whoever she might turn out to be.

"So," Pam said, "obviously we've got to see if it

was something she found out because she was working for you. And that will be in her notes, if anywhere."

It was not obvious to Jerry, holding his head, which ached, that they had to see anything. He said he had seen enough already.

"Stars," Pam said. "I know. It's dreadful, Jerry. But after all, it's your responsibility."

With that, also, Jerry was out of accord. Miss Amelia Gipson was his responsibility only on pay day.

"Employee's compensation," Pam said. "Or insurance. It's a State law. Just as if she had slipped on a rug!"

There was nothing in the State law, Jerry assured her, which made an employer liable for the murder of any of his employees. He looked thoughtful.

"Anyway," he said, "off the premises."

In that case, Pam said, the obligation was all the more pressing, being moral. She looked at Jerry with interested expectancy, waiting obviously for an answer to that one. Jerry looked somewhat puzzled and ran his right hand through his hair.

"Look," he said, "it isn't like tripping on a rug. She didn't fall over anything."

Pam shook her head. She said that was precisely the point. She said she thought Amelia Gipson had fallen over something.

"Something dangerous," she said. "In looking up the old cases. She solved something and the murderer didn't like it." Jerry started to speak. "And I do remember what Bill said," Pam went on. "But I still think it's possible. Didn't Poe?"

"Didn't Poe what," Jerry enquired, incautiously.

"Work out a case the police couldn't solve," Pam said. "Make a story of it?"

That had been fiction, Jerry pointed out. There was no evidence Poe was right. He had a theory, like anyone else; being a man of genius, his theory had been arresting and persuasive. But there was nothing to indicate that it had been right.

"After all," Jerry said, "nobody killed Poe."

"You're getting off the subject," Pam said. "Because your head aches, probably. We were talking about Miss Gipson, whom somebody did kill. We're not trying to solve Poe's death."

Jerry ran a hand through his hair again and smiled suddenly. He said he didn't mind if Pam went through the notes Miss Gipson had made. He said he knew she was going to.

"And," Pam said, "see the writers. Because you say Miss Gipson did. Maybe it was one of them, of course."

"Listen," Gerald North told her, "of all the quiet, peaceable, home bodies, writers of mystery stories. . . ." He broke off.

"All right," he said. "She did see them. Hill, Mrs. Abernathy, the Munroes, Jimmy Robinson. To see if they had any special angles they wanted covered. I suggested it. Robinson is doing the Purdy case; you'll find the others on the notes. And now give me one good reason you should go to see them."

"She did," Pam said. "Whatever she did while she was alive is interesting now because she's dead. Obviously."

Gerald smiled at her contentedly. The Munroes lived in Albany, he pointed out. Did she plan to go to Albany? And Jimmy Robinson had picked up his typewriter and gone South, because he wanted to give cold weather good, and early clearance. And he had not yet sent the office his new address.

There remained Mr. Hill and Mrs. Abernathy, Pam pointed out. And Albany was not impossible, if it proved necessary. The chances were, anyway, that it would all be in the notes.

She was less sure of that, now, having read the notes on the Joyce Wentworth case. If Amelia Gipson had solved that one, she had not hinted at the solution here. Or it was a very evasive hint, too obscure for Pam's detection. She picked up the next of the completed cases.

It was more complex and older. In 1928, a very prosperous family living on a Hudson River estate had been almost wiped out by typhoid fever—typhoid of peculiar, deadly virulence. Agatha Fleming had caught it first, and before she died her husband, Timothy, was violently ill. They had been the old people; Timothy, at seventy-five, had lived only a day or two. Then their elder daughter had become ill and she, too, had died, although after a more protracted illness. The family physician had been frightened by them and called for help. Help had not saved two more of the Flemings— John, who was in his fifties, and Florence, a year or two younger. Florence's husband, however, had recovered after some weeks. The only members of the household, except the servants, to escape entirely were the youngest daughter, Helen, and her husband, Dr. Thomas Merton.

The County, and then the State, authorities sought the source of the infection and failed to find it. And then other authorities, noting that the disease had been oddly selective, assailing only Flemings and leaving others in the house unscathed, and observing that Mrs. Helen Merton now inherited the Fleming fortune, found considerable interest in Dr. Merton's work as a bacteriologist. They also found typhoid cultures— very virulent typhoid cultures—in his laboratory.

The case against Dr. Merton had been, at best, a little speculative. He had, certainly, means and opportunity; it could easily be argued that he had motive. But it was not certain that there had been any crime. He was indicted; he was tried and the trial was long and spectacularly attracted attention. But the jury had not agreed. He was tried again, not for so long a time and with rather less attention from the newspapers, and again the jury failed to reach a decision. (It was reported, however, to have stood nine to three for acquittal.) The State had given it up, then, and the County Medical Association received Dr. Merton back into membership. But his wife had divorced him, after a suitable interval, and the university with which he was connected, after a suitable pause to uphold appearances, had decided not to renew his contract. Dr. Merton had fallen on evil days, which was lamentable if he had not, as the prosecution argued, mixed his typhoid cultures into food consumed by various members of the family.

This case, Pam North decided, was intricate enough. She read Miss Gipson's thorough précis several times. It was clear and detailed; it did not seem, however, to contain any information which, possessed by Miss Gipson, would endanger her life.

Of course, Pam thought, she needn't have written it down. If she found out something—or deduced something—she wouldn't necessarily have put it into notes for—she looked at the first page of the manuscript—Mrs. Abernathy. She might have decided to tell Mrs. Abernathy—or someone else! Pam thought for a moment. "The murderer," she said, aloud this time. "That's what she would do, I should think. Being the kind of person she apparently was. She'd have told the murderer and. . . ."

Now Pam North's mind stopped suddenly and then started up again, faster than ever. Because she saw a coincidence which might be more; because here, in this account of a crime almost twenty years buried, there was a hint, however faint, of modernity.

"Of course," Pam said, "it's a very common name. There must be thousands around. I wonder how old she is?"

Pam North got a sheet of paper and a pencil and began to figure. The answer came out several ways, as answers did when Pam North added to them. But finally she came out with a figure that was, she was pretty sure, right within a year or two. She folded the sheet of paper and stuck it in a pigeonhole. Now she would have to get another figure and see if the two matched.

Pam started to get up and go about other things, which would involve Bill Weigand, but she was stern with herself. The way to do it, she decided, was to be thorough. She still had another case to go through, hunch or no hunch.

Because, of course, that's all it is, Pam told herself. If that.

The third case which Miss Gipson had completed

was no longer a mystery; it had, indeed, been a mystery for only a few hours. Then the police had solved it, to the satisfaction of all but Clara Bright and Thomas Judson, who, a little more than a year after they had killed Clara's husband, died within minutes of each other in Sing Sing Prison. It was difficult, looking at the facts which Miss Gipson had set down with detachment—and somehow a hinted suggestion of disapproval—to see why the Bright-Judson case ever created the sensation it had at the time or why, now, it was thought appropriate to include it in the annals of crime.

Clara Bright and Thomas Judson had been lovers; from the testimony at the trial, they had rather sensationally been lovers. They had killed Henry Bright because he might interfere with their love, although there was little to indicate that he had in fact interfered at all aggressively. Or they had killed Henry Bright because his life was insured for a hundred thousand dollars. Or both. Pam, reading Miss Gipson's summary a second time, thought that Clara had been more interested in the money and Thomas—just possibly more interested in Clara. He had seemed, at any rate, almost pathetically willing to fall into a plan which was almost certainly hers and involved running Bright down with a tractor and, eventually, crushing him against a stone wall. Sordid, unquestionably, Pam decided.

She was struck more than ever on second reading by the attitude which Amelia Gipson had, perhaps unwittingly, displayed toward the whole matter. It was not clear that Miss Gipson was revolted, or even that she was sickened, although the case might revolt or sicken almost anyone. It was more that Miss Gipson disapproved; she seemed, Pam thought, to disapprove of the sexual irregularity involved almost more than she did of the murder. Reading the script, Pam North could imagine that Miss Gipson had washed her hands as she finished each sentence of her notes.

"The evidence showed that, for almost a year before the crime, Clara Bright and Thomas Judson had been involved in a degraded love affair, with the attendant weakening of moral fiber," Pam read. Her eyes widened slightly. She wondered how Miss Gipson knew that there had been an attendant weakening of moral fibre; how she knew that the love affair had been "degraded."

Excessive, maybe, Pam thought. She remembered some of the testimony which had been rather guardedly hinted at in the newspapers. She remembered that she was not then of an age which, in the opinion of her mother, made such reading appropriate and that she had sometimes been put to considerable trouble to get the full story, which *The New York Times* published so extensively under demure headlines. Physical, undoubtedly, she added to herself. But why degraded?

Pam thought about it. Clara and Thomas had, certainly, turned out to be degraded people, and very crude murderers. And their love affair had been, for want of a better term, very physical. But their degradation had been displayed in the murder—in their cold, ruthless hunting down of a harmless, middle-aged man; in their failure to be revolted either by the idea of murder or the actual, and messy, carrying out of murder. How they had comported themselves as lovers was, Pam thought, another matter. They had not, perhaps, been fastidious. They had, certainly, been selfish. They had broken, with a frequency rather overwhelming, the New York statute against adultery.

But "degradation" seemed still a rather stern word. The matter was one of taste. Some people preferred to live one way and not a few people preferred to live much as Clara and Thomas had, this side of murder. It was clear that Miss Gipson disapproved of such and that her disapproval had unexpected violence.

"It's as if she hated—oh, all of it," Pam said, and again she spoke aloud to herself. "Our being animals."

Pam North stood up, almost instinctively, and stretched. She could feel her muscles moving and the silk of the dressing-gown against her skin.

"Really," Pam said, "that was very foolish of her. Because in a way it's fun being animal." She thought.

"Much more than being mineral, I should think," she added. "And certainly than vegetable and always in one place."

She showered, scrubbing herself. It was pleasant to feel clean. That was because of the Bright-Judson case, probably. Or was it, Pam wondered, because of Miss Gipson's attitude toward the Bright-Judson case? It was hard, Pam thought, to determine which seemed the more unwholesome. Fortunately, she thought, putting on a pale green wool dress over nothing in particular, she didn't have to. What she had to do was to get in touch with Bill Weigand. Then, looking at herself in the mirror, she thought of Jerry, as she usually did when she thought she was looking rather nice. Jerry had said not to do anything until she told him first.

Jerry and Pamela North, Bill Weigand and Sergeant Mullins sat, in that order, on bar stools at Charles. Jerry looked tired, and there was a bump on his head; Bill Weigand looked both weary and puzzled; and Mullins stared with a kind of reproach on his face into the glass which had held an old-fashioned. Pam, who looked neither tired nor puzzled, fished the olive out of her martini glass, nibbled it around and said that it oughtn't to be long now before they had Noilly Prat back.

"Otherwise," she said, "it's very much like old times."

"Listen, Pam," Jerry said, earnestly, "there's absolutely no reason to connect the two. It's merely intuition." He considered. "Of a very low order," he added.

Pam said she wished he wouldn't say that. She said intuition had nothing to do with it.

"She'd worked on four cases," Pam pointed out, as if explaining to children. "If we grant that she found out something in one of them that made her dangerous to somebody, where are we?"

Bill Weigand said to wait a minute. He said they didn't grant it. He said they had no real reason to think it.

"We have," he pointed out, "at least two people who profit by her death. Her nephew and niece. We have a man—a rather odd duck—she had got thrown out of a job, with the result that he's gone to pot. We may have half a dozen other things. Real things, Pam."

"Sometimes," Pam said, "I think you think money is the root of all murder."

Bill was undisturbed. He said it usually was. He said it almost always was except when murder was sudden, violent, unpremeditated.

"Money," he said, "or safety. Which are very often the same thing. Certainly, it's the first place to look."

That was all right, Pam agreed. She said that if he widened it that much—put in safety—it would still cover her theory.

"Because," she said, "my theory supposes Miss Gipson became dangerous to the safety of a person who was already a murderer. In this case, an unsuspected one."

"Yours isn't a theory, Pam," Jerry said. "It's a leap. Out of the dark; into the dark."

As for that, Bill said, rather unexpectedly, anything they did now was a leap. They leaped at one person and then at another; at one possibility and then at another. The trouble, he said, was not that Pam was leaping. It was that she was leaping without a target.

"Nevertheless," Pam said, "you can't simply ignore the letter. It has to be explained. I merely want to go along, and I think we ought to go today. And all I want, really, is to find out how old she is. If she's the wrong age, the whole thing goes out the window."

Mullins spoke suddenly.

"There's always the inspector, loot," he said. "Ain't there?"

"Right," Bill said. "There's always the inspector, Pam."

"The trouble with the inspector," Pam said, "one of the troubles, is that he thinks murder is a private affair. It isn't. I'm a citizen and she worked for Jerry."

Bill smiled. He said he hadn't forgotten that. He said he supposed they could use it again, if necessary.

"How is Inspector O'Malley?" Pam wanted to know. "Does he still think it was suicide?"

Weigand said the inspector was weakening. He said the inspector was ready now to settle for murder, if he could have Philip Spencer for murderer.

"I like Spencer," Mullins said. "It's sorta reasonable."

Bill Weigand said he didn't dislike Spencer. He said it was too early to like anybody.

"How about the girl?" Jerry said. "The maid. What was her name?"

Weigand told him it was Florence Adams. He said they hadn't heard anything about her.

"Run out powder," Mullins said, fishing out a half slice of orange and munching it ruminatively. "Or she could of known too much."

"She could of," Bill agreed. "She probably did— does. She'll probably turn up."

Hugo came and said their table was ready, and that he was sorry. He said things ought to get better now, with the war over. They went back through the crowded restaurant to the table. Things were getting better, Pam said. Consider butter.

They considered butter, and other things. After they had finished and were standing up, Pam North looked at Bill and raised her arched eyebrows. Bill smiled.

"Right," he said. "As you say, the letter has to be explained."

6

Wednesday, 1:30 P.M. to 1:33 P.M.

We use kinder words about ourselves than others use; we do not see or hear about ourselves what others see. Florence Adams could have read the police description of herself and, with the name omitted, found that it stirred no faintest recollection of anyone she had ever seen. Her skin was rather dark, and she thought of it as "olive"; her hair was black, surely, but the word "black" alone did not describe it—it would have been, had been, a word which, used alone, was clearly inadequate for the purpose. She had read, in a magazine story, of a heroine whose hair was "lustrous black" and, although Florence Adams could not readily have told how a lustrous thing would look, she thought afterward of her own hair as like the heroine's in the book. Magazines were books to Florence Adams, as they were, at the other extreme, to magazine editors.

Florence Adams was a slight, not tall, girl—perhaps *petite* was the word—with lustrous black hair and an olive complexion. She wore a close-fitting, two-piece dress of autumn-leaf brown, and her black eyes, also, were more than merely black. There was depth to them—as, indeed, there had been to the eyes of her heroine in the book. She almost never wore glasses, since she wore glasses only when she read. No one would have thought of her as myopic; she never thought of herself as myopic, never having heard the word. That was—that partly was—Florence Adams to Florence Adams. If she would not have recognized herself from the police description, the police surely would not have recognized her from her own.

Nobody else had recognized Florence from the police description by one o'clock Wednesday afternoon. A great many people had seen her, or could have seen her. Actually, it is improbable that many did see her— see her clearly enough, consciously enough, to know that her complexion was sallow-olive, her hair black, her dress a rather muddy brown; that she was—or would be if she lived long enough—rather top-heavy; that she did not use color on her fingernails, although this last was faintly noteworthy. Those who saw her at all saw a small young woman of no particular appearance in clothes of no particular color, and would have assumed—if they had troubled—that she was going nowhere in particular. In this last, at any rate, they would have been wrong.

Florence had gone to a movie Tuesday night and had sat, obediently, through both features. She had never left a motion picture theater in her life without seeing all of both pictures; it would never have occurred to her that this was possible. She had therefore been on upper Broadway at about midnight and had bought a copy of *The Daily News*. She had gone into an all-night drugstore to read it and have a cup of coffee; she had got to the story of Miss Gipson's death after she had finished the comics and while she was looking idly at the rest of the paper, chiefly at the pictures. The name had leaped out at her and she had sat a moment staring at it. Then she had gone home, almost running. Because then she was frightened and wanted familiar walls around her.

But when she stopped to think—when she stopped to look around, anxiously, at the familiar walls—they did not offer the sanctuary they had promised. It was, this small room, the first place they would come. She was cold, suddenly, although the night was warm; involuntarily she shivered. They would come; at any moment they would come. And with her fear there was a sharp, violent anger. Words of hate, of description, came to her mind which she could not have, if she had been able to analyze—if she had had the habit of analysis—remembered she had ever heard. Certainly she had never used them.

So it was not an easy way of earning a hundred dollars, enough for a new winter coat and to spare. It was a way to get the police after her; to get herself put in prison. Or—her mind balked at the alternative. But her mind could not shake off the alternative. They killed people who killed other people—who even helped kill other people. She trembled; she listened with a kind of terrified intensity. And then she knew she had to get away.

She had not many clothes to pack in an old suitcase, but there were too many when she added the coat. She did not need the coat, so she left it hanging in the room. She tried to take everything; tried to obliterate all trace of herself in the room, but she did not think of the opened newspaper as a trace. She turned off the light after she had finished packing and opened the door to the hall fearfully and looked up and down the corridor. There were only dim lights in the hall and there was no one to see her, yet as she went she walked close to the wall and made herself small. There was something protective about a wall.

It was desperately hard to step out into the street, and for a moment she hesitated, shrinking, in the doorway. She must not look as if she were frightened, as if she were running away. But, lugging her suitcase up the street toward Broadway, looking around her at a world which always—because she did not need to wear glasses, really, unless she was reading—was half shrouded in fog, she looked only like a frightened girl running away. She looked younger than she had for a good many years; the shell which had protected her, as a shell might protect some small helpless animal, had dissolved. Any perceptive person would have noticed this, and a policeman might have. But she did not see any policeman on her way to the subway at 110th Street, and none saw her.

The subway was familiar. Every day, at a little after nine in the morning, she entered at this place and rode down to the Sheridan Square station, from which she could walk to the Holborn Annex. She rode on the local, if that came first, to Ninety-sixth Street. If she were lucky, and an express came first, she rode straight through. Otherwise she changed at Ninety-sixth. She rode the express to Fourteenth Street and changed to the local and rode one stop to Sheridan Square. It was familiar.

Now she had to wait for a train longer than in the mornings, but even as she waited the sense of familiarity grew. There was protection here, on the almost empty platform, which her room had not offered. People looked at her incuriously; she had the consciousness of their glances passing over her and not hesitating. She did not put the confidence this gave her into words, but she knew that there could not be anything so changed about her. She even looked at herself in the mirror of one of the machines which vended chewing gum and, after she had looked, straightened her hat and powdered her nose. She was much calmer—much less frightened—when the train came and she entered it, and was engulfed by the familiar, reassuring, metallic roar of its progress through the tunnel.

It was a local and she changed at Ninety-sixth, almost unconsciously following the familiar pattern. But as the express racketed downtown, she began to think what she would do; where she would go. At first she thought of going to some other city where nobody knew her. She could not achieve the realization that, even in New York, where she had been born, she was known to almost no one. It did not surprise her that she knew no one well enough to go to them and explain—or perhaps partly explain—what had happened and ask them for help. Her parents were both dead; there was an aunt in Brooklyn, she almost never saw her and did not like her and was not liked by her. She had never had any permanent association with a man in her life; she had gone to movies with boys, and to dinner a few times, but none of the boys, except Fred, had reappeared after one, or at the most two, dates. And Fred was still in the Navy, and she did not think that Fred would remember her, although he had more cause to remember her than had any other man she had ever known. But she did not remember him very clearly either, in spite of what had happened, and did not feel any particular resentment. The two other women who worked as maids at the Holborn Annex were much older and they were foreigners and spoke funny English, so that she had never thought much about them. So there was no one. And yet she had to go somewhere.

She still did not regret leaving her room; that, clearly, had been the only thing to do. That would be the first place they would go and she had to avoid them at any cost. Just now, at any rate. And for the same reason she had to stay away from the Holborn Annex, which was the second place they would go. The thing she had to do was to find some place to spend the rest of the night. She thought, for a moment, that she might spend it in the subway, riding back and forth. But someone might notice; and, almost certainly, there would be drunks. It would be cheaper, but she had a lot of money. More than a hundred dollars, because she had not touched the hundred and she must have four or five. She counted in her mind. She had four dollars and twenty cents—no, fifteen cents, because the subway had taken a nickel—in addition to the hundred. Enough for anything she could think of. She could live a long time on that—anyway, until she found another job. She could even go to a hotel.

This idea came to her slowly, because it was not an idea she had ever had before, or thought of having. You found a room somewhere in a rooming house; even if you wanted the room for only a short time, you found it in a rooming house. But it was late to go looking for a room as you always did. Hotels, she supposed, were not surprised if people came in in the middle of the night and asked for a room. Probably people did that every night, and hotels expected it.

Forty-second Street and Broadway was the most likely place to find a room, she thought; it was the center of the city. She got off at Forty-second Street and came up into the lights. Everything was bright again now, with the war over. Probably Fred would be coming back soon. She thought of this, fleetingly and without reference to herself. He would not be coming back to her. It did not matter particularly; she had not greatly enjoyed her experiences with Fred. In a way it had been exciting, but he was drunk most of the time and everything had been abrupt and, somehow, had seemed unfinished. Perhaps that was the way it always was.

She walked west on Forty-second Street, looking for a hotel, because she supposed there must be hotels on Forty-second Street. She went across Eighth Avenue, knowing that the kind of hotel she wanted would probably be west of Eighth Avenue and, very quickly, found a hotel. There was a door with a marquee marked "Hotel" and there was no sign which limited the accommodations to men. Beyond the door was a flight of stairs, with brass edges on the treads, and at the top of the stairs were two glass doors, swinging together and both marked "Hotel." Inside there was a desk; and the old man at it, who smelled a little, told her without interest that she could have a room for two dollars, and took the two dollars. He told her where to find the room, and she went along a dirty hall—the whole place smelled a little, like the clerk—until she found a room with the right number on the door. She went in and turned on the light. The room looked very much like the room she had lived in uptown, and she thought nobody would find her there until she was ready to be found.

She undressed, after locking the door, and thought about what she would do. She would not do anything until morning, she decided, but then she would do something. She'd sure do something. Nobody was going to put her on a spot this way and get away with it.

Her anger, which had been smouldering as a kind of

bitterness, flared up as she thought about the person who had put her on the spot. The story might have taken anybody in—the story that Miss Gipson had stolen some papers and was hiding them in her room. She had read about that happening in one of the books she read and was not surprised. (Florence, if she had thought about it, probably would have realized that the stories she read in her books were things people had made up. But she always read them with the belief that they were things which had actually happened.)

Since papers might be of any conceivable value, it was not surprising that the offer for her key—for the few hours' possession of her key—had amounted to a hundred dollars. Sums like that were commonplace in cases where people wanted to get at papers, and Miss Gipson was precisely the sort of person who would steal papers from their rightful owners and refuse to return them. Miss Gipson was a bitch. Florence remembered that Miss Gipson was dead and changed the word in her mind. Miss Gipson had been—been hard to get along with. She had been snoopy about her room, always running the tips of her fingers along the least likely places in search of dust. She had several times behaved as if she thought Florence might steal something. She was dead, but she had not been a very nice lady, all the same.

But she was dead, and Florence had been put on a spot because she had been lied to, and nobody was going to get away with that. If she had to, she would go to the police and tell them about it, and explain that she had been taken in by a story that anybody would have believed, because if she was going to be on a spot, somebody else was going to be there too. They'd see.

Florence Adams had felt safe with the door locked, and having made up her mind what she was going to do. She had gone to sleep after a much shorter time than anybody would have expected, and she had slept until after ten o'clock. Then she had gone out to breakfast and come back in an hour and read the newspapers. It was after eleven when she went down and made her telephone call.

At first, she had had a little trouble making the person who had put her on the spot realize who she was.

"Florence Adams," she said, and said it several times. "The maid at the Holborn Annex. Where Miss Gipson lived."

It had been clear, then, and Florence had gone at once to the point.

"You put me on the spot," she said. "You can't get away with it. I'm going to the police."

She listened for a time.

"I'd like to see you prove it," she said then, skeptically. "You could get into her place. And somebody planted this poison—sodium something—there. It was worth a hundred bucks to you to get into the place. That's a lot of money."

She listened again.

"Listen," she said, "there isn't that much money. You think I want to be locked up? Or worse? I—"

The voice at the other end of the wire broke in, and this time Florence listened for a longer period, although once or twice she started to break in. When the voice finally finished, Florence hesitated a moment.

"You make it sound all right," she said, and there was uncertainty in her voice. "You made it sound all right the other time. What do you want me to do?"

"Let me talk to you," the voice said. "You're making a mistake. You'll get yourself into trouble—needlessly." The voice was slow, demanding attention and belief. "When you hear the full story you'll realize that there is no connection between the two things. I did not kill Miss Gipson. I'm sure I can make you understand that. Only you must let me talk to you before you go to the police."

"Well—" Florence said.

"It will be worth your while," the voice said. "In more ways than one. You will see that you have nothing to reproach yourself with. And I won't forget

what you do. It is quite true that it is worth a good deal
to me not to be involved in any way."

Florence Adams had thought for a moment, and
what the voice said seemed reasonable. After all, the
other was—was something that happened only in stories, like love different from that she had known with
Fred; like inheriting a million dollars from an unknown
uncle in Australia. It was to be expected that there
would be an ordinary explanation.

"All right," she said. "I'll come and see you"

She listened again.

"Well," she said, "it's not much of a place. It's
called Freeman's Hotel and it's in Forty-second Street
between Eighth and Ninth. But it doesn't matter to
me. I'll go back and wait for you."

She had listened to the voice again.

"All right," she said. "But you don't need to go to
the bank. If it's like you say, I won't tell the police.
You don't have to give me any more money."

Again she listened.

"If you feel that way," she said. "I could use it. I'll
probably have to get a new job because I missed today
anyway. Only you don't have to."

She had listened once more, this time briefly, and
hung up the receiver. She had felt much better; that
strange feeling of having done something wrong had
left her. She had frightened herself for no reason.
Suddenly she was lighthearted. Everything was fine.
She had a hundred dollars and was going to have more
and she would get a new job—perhaps a better job.
And maybe she would meet Fred again, or someone
better than Fred—someone with whom she would
have more fun, someone who would be nicer to her,
act more as if she were somebody to be thought of.
And today she had nothing to do.

She had looked at the clock in the drugstore from
which she had telephoned and it had been only about
11:30. She had walked over to Broadway and up to
Forty-seventh and then down on the other side,
merely looking at things. It was a bright, warm day
and people were out on the streets and the movies

were open. She thought of going to a movie, but decided she would not have time. She felt very well and happy, as if the night had merely been a dream she had forgotten.

She had gone to a chop suey restaurant at about 12:30, and the chop suey had been very good. It was a little after 1:00 when she went back to her room at the hotel, because she did not want to be late.

The room was not on the side of the hotel which got the sun, if any side did. After the bright world outdoors, the room seemed dark and somehow grimy. The window, Florence Adams saw, opened on an air shaft, so the room could not have been sunny whatever side of the building it was on. But she would not have to stay there much longer. As soon as the talk was over she would go out where it was bright again, and then she would look for another room. A better room than she had had uptown, or than this; a room with sun in it.

The person with whom she had made her appointment was prompt. Florence had been back in the room only a few minutes when there was a knock on the door. She got up from the bed on which she had been sitting and went across and opened the door, smiling.

"Come in," she said. "I told you it wasn't—"

And then, seeing what was in the visitor's hand and seeing also what was in the visitor's eyes, she began to walk backward into the room and she tried to speak. She tried to scream, but something was catching at her throat.

She did not make any sound until the door had closed behind the visitor, and then she would not have known her own voice.

"No!" she said, her voice was shrill and seemed to crack, but the volume of sound was very small. *"No! You can't!* You can't! You—"

But Florence Adams was wrong about that. The noise was loud in the little room, but she did not hear it. The hotel was almost empty, because most of the people who lived in it were at work. And the room was, by a chance lucky for no one except the murderer, a long way from the little lobby. The clerk was old and tired, and did not hear very well, and to him the sound was dismissed as the backfire from a truck. It was dismissed so completely that he could not afterward remember it at all.

But it would not have made any real difference to Florence Adams if he had heard it clearly for what it was; if he had been young and dangerous and had come running. It would not have made any difference to her who had come, or how quickly.

7

They had split up after lunch at Charles. Jerry had gone back to his office, looking doubtfully at Pam as he left; looking as though he expected little good to come of this. Mullins had gone to the law offices of Williams, Franke and Backley, to find out what he could from Mr. Backley, presuming he could find Mr. Backley. Pamela North and Weigand had gone to Weigand's office, on their way to visit with Mrs. Willard Burt, who had been in cryptic correspondence with Amelia Gipson. Bill Weigand wanted to see what had come in on Mrs. Burt before they discovered what could be got out of Mrs. Burt.

There was more to do than that; more grist to consider. There was an answer to his telegraphed request for further information on Philip Spencer; there was the report of a precinct man that Mr. Spencer was apparently remaining obediently at home. There were reports on some of the men and women, boys and girls, who had happened to be reading in the New York Public Library when Miss Gipson drank poison there—if she did drink poison there.

Pam, waiting, asked for and got Miss Gipson's notebook on the Purdy case. It did not tell much more than she already knew; it did not tell as much as she already knew. The police had kept a secret or two for future use. She read that Mrs. Purdy had been taken suddenly ill after drinking a glass of water which should have had bicarbonate of soda in solution, Mrs. Purdy

81

being momentarily troubled by gas. The water had, in fact, sodium fluoride in solution, which Mrs. Purdy might have noticed in time if she had not drunk the water off very rapidly because she disliked the flavor of bicarbonate of soda. She had lived longer than Miss Gipson had, Pam noticed; it had been almost eight hours before Mrs. Purdy had died. Pam supposed the dose had been smaller.

It was not clear from Miss Gipson's notes what had aroused the suspicions of the police, so Pam supposed that it had not been clear in the newspaper stories. But from the start, the police had been questioning Mr. Purdy about the death of his wife. They had never seemed impressed by the theory of accident, although admittedly the box which contained the poison had been generally similar to that which contained the soda and admittedly they had been kept close together—too close together, one would have thought—on a kitchen shelf. It was, to be sure, difficult to see how Mrs. Purdy would have made even more difficult mistakes, with similarly fatal results, without invoking serious police enquiry.

Miss Gipson had noted the oddity, here, and commented on it for her author. "Apparently police had additional info. not disclosed," she had written, no doubt for future amplification. It was, incidentally, one of the last things she had written about the case. There was the additional fact that Purdy had disappeared; that he had been traced to the airport and aboard a plane, and that the plane had crashed and burned a few hundred miles short of Los Angeles. His body, badly burned, had been identified by unburned possessions—a ring, a wrist watch, keys. There the case had ended. It did not, Pamela thought, offer much to a writer, but you could never tell about writers. Jerry said as much, sometimes aggrievedly. If there had not been money involved—if Mrs. Purdy had not been a very rich woman, and Mr. Purdy an only moderately well-to-do man, and if he had not stood to inherit largely—the newspapers would hardly, Mrs. North thought, have given the matter much attention.

Miss Gipson had revealed the final disposal of Mr. Purdy, had started a new sentence in her firm script and then had broken off to write: "I have been poisoned by—" in script which remained firm until the down stroke of the "*y*." That stroke had continued, wavering, down the notebook page; it had ended, one could guess, when Miss Gipson's hand would no longer obey her mind. Nothing in the Purdy case was half so interesting, so dramatic, as this unfinished record of it.

Pam put the notebook down and looked at Bill Weigand, who was looking at her and waiting.

"It was a strange coincidence," she said.

Bill nodded. He said there seemed to be a good many coincidences. Spencer's presence, if it was a coincidence. Mrs. Burt's first name, since Pam would have it that way. Pam nodded.

"Only," she said, "when you come down to it, there always are. Like meeting people on the street and having them telephone you when you're thinking about them. Like speak of the devil and that sort of thing."

Bill said he still distrusted them. He said that he was ready to go see Mrs. Burt now.

"Chiefly," he said, "because Miss Gipson's niece and her brother have gone to LaGuardia to meet the girl's husband. There's—well, there's no use breaking that up since we don't have to."

"And," Pam said, "you want to wait until Mullins talks to the lawyer, Mr. Backley. Although I don't say you wouldn't just as soon be considerate, if everything else was even. Did they identify?"

John Gipson had identified his aunt's body, Bill told her. He had said that they both, he and his sister, wanted to help; he had explained that Major Kennet Frost was due in that afternoon and that his sister was keyed up, her feelings hopelessly confused, and in no condition to be coherent.

"After all," he had said, "her aunt murdered; her husband coming back after more than two years in the Pacific. It's a lot for twenty-four hours."

Gipson was willing, he made it clear, to talk to the police at any time. He also, it was equally clear, wanted to go with his sister to the airport.

"And," Bill said, "actually we were in no hurry."

"Backley," Pamela repeated. "Shall we go? And what about Mrs. Burt?"

Bill told her what they had found out about Mrs. Burt on their way to the Burt apartment. She was a woman in her late forties; she had been a widow until about two years before, when she had married Willard Burt. Apparently she had had money before she married; apparently Burt also was well-to-do. They had come east from California some months after their marriage. They had lived in an apartment on Park Avenue for a few weeks less than a year. He stopped with that. Pam said they didn't know a great deal.

"We'll know more," Bill told her. "No answer yet from California." He smiled at her. "Frankly, Pam," he said, "it doesn't take precedence."

"I know it's a hunch," she said. "And don't call it intuition, Bill. She could be the right age, however."

The world, Bill pointed out, was full of people the right age.

"Only one of whom wrote a letter," Pam told him. "Don't quibble, Bill."

It was clear he was not quibbling, Bill said, because there they were. The letter needed explanation; they had come to get the explanation.

"Can I ask my questions?" Pam wanted to know.

Bill shook his head as he held out a hand to assist her from the police car. Pam made polite acknowledgment of the hand by waving in its direction, which was all that either of them expected. She made polite acknowledgment of the shaking head by saying, "All right, Bill, then you do," and they went into the apartment house.

It was very elegant, in a curiously antique fashion. It had been built in expansive days. They entered a colonnaded expanse, too large to be called a lobby. There were concrete arches in various directions; there were concrete seats, faintly Grecian, with red cushions on them. A very ancient doorman got up from one of the seats and advanced as if he were moving to funeral music. They asked for directions to the Willard Burt apartment.

He did not answer, but he did point. He pointed as if he were tired of pointing. They sighted with his finger and saw, in the subdued distance, among the colonnades, another old man in a green uniform—but without golden epaulets—sitting, evidently asleep, on another red cushion on another concrete bench. They went, Pam's high heels clicking between the scattered rugs. The man was not asleep, or not quite asleep. He was guarding a tiny elevator. He got up when they were very close and looked at them.

"The Burts," Bill Weigand said, his voice unconsciously muted.

The man did not answer, but he waved them toward the elevator. They got in and he got in, and the three of them filled it.

"Listen," Pam said, "this is a dreadful bottleneck. For such a big place and everything."

The elevator man did not seem to hear her.

"There are other elevators," Bill told her, his voice still hushed.

The elevator stopped at the fifth floor. The elevator man waited and they got out.

"There are ten elevators," the man said in measured tones, shut the grill door, and went down.

"I feel," Pam said, "as if we should have sent flowers, don't you, Bill?"

There was only one door to consider. Bill pushed a button, and chimes came faintly from within. After a pause a middle-aged maid came to the door and looked at them politely.

"Mrs. Burt?" Bill said. He did not wait for the question he could see forming. "Lieutenant Weigand, of the police," he said. "You might tell her it is fairly important."

"The police?" the maid said. She sounded very surprised.

"Yes," Bill said. "If you don't mind."

"I don't know if she's in," the maid said. "She was out." She looked at them doubtfully. "If you'll come in, I'll see," she said. She still seemed very doubtful and surprised.

The foyer was larger than many rooms, but it was gay and bright with chintz, and there were flowers on a table. There was a seat for two, and they sat on it. The maid came back after only a minute or two.

"Mrs. Burt has just come in," she said. "If you will come this way?"

They went that way. They went into an enormous living room, with a fireplace—with white chairs and green chairs and yellow chairs; with many glowing lamps and with a middle-aged woman standing near the center.

"Mr. Weigand," the maid said. "He says he's from the police. And—" She looked at Mrs. North, who was unexplained.

"Mrs. North," Bill said, not explaining. "Mrs. Burt?"

"Do come in," Mrs. Burt said. "Do come in and sit down, Mr. Weigand. And Mrs.—" She let the last trail off. She spoke in a light, quick voice, as if she were excited. She was a gray-haired woman, slight and rather pretty; a few years ago she must have been very pretty. There was softness and fragility about her, and a kind of eagerness. She motioned them to one of two facing sofas and, when they were in front of it, sat down opposite them. They sat down.

"I am investigating the death of Miss Amelia Gipson," Bill said. "You've probably read about it?"

"Oh yes," Mrs. Burt said, and there was a kind of eagerness in her voice, as if she were pleased to be able to make the right answer. "Dear Amelia. I'm so sorry. So terribly sorry. We were girls together, you know."

"Yes," Weigand said, "I gathered that from your letter, Mrs. Burt."

She looked puzzled. But before she looked puzzled expression seemed to flicker out in her eyes and return again.

"My letter?" she said. "What letter?"

Bill Weigand was patient. He said the one she had written to Miss Gipson. On Monday, he presumed.

"Oh," Mrs. Burt said. "Oh yes, of course. That letter."

"You understand, Mrs. Burt," Bill said, "we have to find out everything we can in a case of sudden death. We have to look into many things which are probably irrelevant. Like your letter. You understand that?"

"Oh, yes," Mrs. Burt said. "Of course, Mr.—what was your name? I'm so dreadful about names."

"Weigand," Bill told her. "Lieutenant Weigand."

"Of course," Mrs. Burt said. "Oh, of course. How stupid of me."

She seemed content with that, and looked at him with a kind of fluttering anxiety, waiting for him to go on; anxious to help him in a situation, her manner implied, he must obviously find difficult.

"About the letter," Bill said, after waiting a moment. "My superiors, Mrs. Burt, seem to feel that it may—indirectly, of course—help us in some fashion." He smiled pleasantly. "If you remember," he said, "you wrote of some mistake you felt Miss Gipson had made. You called it a terrible mistake. And you asked her to trust you."

"Oh," Mrs. Burt said. "That?"

"Right," Bill said. "Naturally, I think, we wondered whether the mistake Miss Gipson had made—the terrible mistake—could have anything to do with her death."

"Oh no," Mrs. Burt said, quickly. "Oh no, lieutenant. This was quite a personal thing."

"Was it?" Bill said.

"Oh, it was," Mrs. Burt told him, with the same eagerness she had shown since the beginning. "It was quite a personal thing.

"I'm afraid you've had so much trouble for nothing, lieutenant," she said. "I'm so sorry."

She moved forward on the sofa, as if she expected

the two across from her to rise, now, and go away. But
Weigand merely nodded.

"I was sure it was," he said. "That was always my
view, Mrs. Burt. But my superiors—"

"Oh," Mrs. Burt said. "That's perfectly all right. I
understand perfectly."

Bill waited politely while she spoke and then nodded
again.

"My superiors," he said, "will, I'm afraid, want to
know what the personal thing was, Mrs. Burt." He
smiled at her, it seemed to Pam North deprecatingly. It
occurred to her she had never seen Bill in quite this
mood before. "You understand how thorough we have
to be," he said to Mrs. Burt. "Digging into all sorts of
things which don't really concern us, just to make sure
they don't. In murder, Mrs. Burt."

His voice was suddenly deeper, more forceful, on
the last words. He did not pause.

"So I'm afraid I'll have to be inquisitive," he said.
"What was the personal thing you were alluding to in
your letter to Miss Gipson, Mrs. Burt? What were you
and she going to talk about tomorrow."

"Really!" Mrs. Burt said. "Oh, really!"

Bill Weigand merely looked at her. His look waited.

"Oh," Mrs. Burt said. "Must I?"

"I'm afraid so," Bill said. "We can't force you to
tell us anything, Mrs. Burt—not here. But we could
consider it very—strange—if you insisted on keeping
it secret."

"Oh," Mrs. Burt said. "But it's nothing. Really
nothing. A foolish thing between poor Amelia and
me." She broke off and her eyes filled, or seemed to
fill, with tears. "And now there will never be a chance
to explain," she said. "Oh—why do people?"

She looked at Bill and Pam North as if she expected
an answer. Pam shook her head; Bill merely waited.

"Somebody had told Amelia dreadful things about
me," Mrs. Burt said, and now she spoke in a rush.
"That I'd said terrible things about her, I mean—about
Amelia. And of course I hadn't—I couldn't. It was all
some terrible mistake."

"What things?" Bill said.

"Oh, I didn't," Mrs. Burt said. "I didn't say anything about Amelia. Why would I?"

There was no answer to that. But Bill amplified.

"What were the things that Miss Gipson had been led to think you had said about her?" he asked.

Mrs. Burt shook her head.

"Oh, it was all confused," she said. "And I was so upset and worried—and—oh, so terribly upset. Something about my having said that she was cruel to her niece. To Nora, you know? And had tried to break things up between Nora and her husband. But I never said anything of the kind. I never *thought* anything of the kind—the idea never—It was some terrible misunderstanding."

"Who had told her you had said that?" Bill wanted to know.

Mrs. Burt shook her head.

"She wouldn't tell me," she said. "She said it wasn't fair to tell me, but that she'd talk to whoever it was and tell them what I said. But she didn't—at least she didn't come back and talk to me again, as she promised. And so I wrote her."

She stopped and looked at Bill Weigand and Pamela North and it was almost certain that there were tears in her eyes.

"She died thinking that about me!" Helen Burt said. "I'm sure she did. That I was telling lies about her. It's so—so terrible."

Bill Weigand looked at her a moment before he spoke.

"And that was all of it?" he said. "That was all the letter was about?"

"Oh yes," Mrs. Burt said. "Oh yes, lieutenant."

"I see," Bill said. "But what did you mean wasn't safe? You wrote 'It isn't safe for either of us,' or words like that. What wasn't safe?"

"Oh," Mrs. Burt said. "That! I mean—I only meant that it wasn't safe for our friendship. We had been such friends for so long—ever since we were girls. I meant it wasn't safe for that not to clear things up."

For a moment more Weigand said nothing. Then he said, "Right. I see, Mrs. Burt." Then he said:

"By the way, were you girls together here? In New York?

"Oh yes," Mrs. Burt said. "Here. And at school. And in the summers."

"In Maine?" Weigand said. "I understand the Gipsons used to spend their summers in Maine."

"In Maine," Mrs. Burt said. "Oh, yes. When we—" She interrupted herself and looked beyond them at the door through which they had come. "Why, Willard," she said. "I thought you—" She seemed surprised.

Willard Burt was in his middle fifties; he was also of middle height. He wore rimless glasses. He wore a gray suit which picked up his gray hair and a gray tie just flecked with yellow. He was very quiet and unhurried, standing in the door of his living room. He smiled at his wife and his smile took in, in anticipation of an introduction, the two sitting across from her. When he spoke it was slowly, with almost studied calm; it was as if his words, his manner, were supports for his wife's unsteadiness.

"Good afternoon, my dear," he said. "I realize you thought I would be later. But I found there was no need." He smiled again, easily. "If I'm interrupting?" he said, the words evenly spaced, the unfinished sentence finished by his calm.

"Oh, Willard," Mrs. Burt said. "I'm so sorry. This is Lieutenant Weigand and this is Mrs.—Mrs. North. I think it is Mrs. North, isn't it, my dear?"

"North," Pam told her. "Mrs. Gerald North. I'm— my husband and I are friends of Lieutenant Weigand."

"Oh, of course," Mrs. Burt said, as her husband nodded slowly and smiled again and said, "Good afternoon." "Of course, my dear. Lieutenant Weigand is from the police, Willard. About poor Amelia. Some foolish letter I wrote, and they wanted explained. Isn't that it, lieutenant?"

Weigand was standing up and facing Willard Burt. He said, "Right." He said, "Good afternoon, Mr. Burt." He said he was sorry to have bothered Mrs.

Burt and that they were just going. Mr. Burt said it was very sad about poor Miss Gipson.

"She and my wife were great friends in the old days," he said. "Very great friends. Weren't you, my dear?"

"Oh yes," Mrs. Burt said. "Such great friends, Willard."

"I hope, lieutenant, that my wife's explanation was—coherent?"

Willard Burt smiled beyond Weigand as he spoke, his smile one of tender apology for the question.

"Quite coherent," Bill assured him. "Entirely coherent and complete, Mr. Burt. As I told Mrs. Burt, it was merely one of the minor details on which my superiors thought it wise to check."

"Naturally," Mr. Burt said. "I didn't know about the letter, of course. But if there was one which was not entirely—shall I say, self-explanatory?—you had to satisfy yourselves. It is a very sad thing, Miss Gipson's death."

"Very," Weigand agreed. Pam North was standing beside him.

"Oh Mrs. Burt," she said, "did you ever know Mrs. Merton? Mrs. Helen Merton? I ask because there was a Mrs. Merton who was a great friend of my mother and she knew a Mrs. Burt. Several years ago and I—" She stopped, because Mrs. Burt was shaking her head.

"No, Mrs. North," she said. "I never knew a Mrs. Merton that I can recall. And I couldn't have been the right Mrs. Burt, of course, because I've only been Mrs. Burt for—how long is it, dear?"

"Less than two years, my dear," Mr. Burt said, in his calm, quiet voice. "Twenty-two months, to be exact."

"Oh," Pam said, "then it couldn't have been, of course. This was much longer ago. In—oh, it was years ago. In 1928, I think. That my mother knew Mrs. Merton, I mean."

Both of the Burts looked at Pam North. They were politely detached and curious.

"It was some other Mrs. Burt," Pam said. "I remember, now. That Mrs. Burt's husband was a doctor. And you're *Mr.* Burt."

"An investor," Mr. Burt said. "Purely an investor, Mrs. North."

The Burts stood side by side as they watched Bill Weigand and Pamela North go out of the room, and heard the door closed behind them.

"You must tell me about the letter, my dear," Willard Burt said to his wife, in his slow, calm voice.

Bill Weigand could see that Pam was excited. She spoke almost as the door closed behind them, but her voice was low.

"Bill!" she said. "Did you get it?"

He nodded slowly.

"That Mrs. Burt uses Fleur de Something or Other?"

He said. "Yes, Pam."

"Well?" Pam said, as he pressed the button for the elevator.

"It's interesting," he said. "Several things were interesting."

The elevator came. It took them down. They walked through the colonnades.

"Her story about the letter," Pam said. "Was that interesting?"

"Very," Bill said. His voice was dry.

"True?" Pam said.

"Not very," Bill told her. "I shouldn't think it was very true, Pam. Your Merton stuff was very subtle."

"Well," Pam said, "it isn't easy to bring in. I couldn't just say, 'By the way, Mrs. Burt, while we're on the subject of murder, are you the divorced wife of Dr. Thomas Merton, who was tried and not quite convicted of killing a whole family in 1928? But was it really you who killed them, and not your husband at all, and did Miss Amelia Gipson find that out somehow in digging into the old case and did you kill her so she couldn't tell the police?' Could I?"

"No," Bill said, "probably not."

"Did you watch her when I mentioned the name?" Pam said. "And what did you think?"

"Yes," Bill said. "And I don't know. Did you think she'd faint? Or confess on the spot?"

"I thought she would—show something," Pam said. "In her face. And—I don't know. Her eyes—did she seem to go away, for a second?"

Bill Weigand held open the door of the police car and Pam got in.

"It's hard to tell," he said. "There—could have been something."

"It was *Helen* Merton," Pam said. "And she'd be about Mrs. Burt's age and—"

Bill nodded slowly. He said he thought they'd try to find out, for the record, what had happened to Mrs. Merton after she had divorced her husband a noncommittal few months after he was just not convicted of murdering her father and mother, two of her sisters and a brother. When he finished saying that he looked, not as if he were seeing anything, at the back of the detective who was driving the car. His face was very thoughtful.

Then the radio, which had been droning in a monotone, spoke sharply.

"Car Forty call in," it said. "Car Forty call in. This is urgent. That is all."

The car swerved toward a cigar store on the next corner. Pam North and the driver waited in the car while Weigand went in. They looked at him when he came out, a few minutes later. His face was more than thoughtful now. It was angry.

"They got the maid," he said, and his voice was angry. "Shot her in a cheap hotel in Forty-second Street. I suppose she tried a shakedown." He got into the car. "The poor little fool," he said. "The poor, pathetic little fool!"

8

Florence Adams had been shot once and the bullet had gone in just above the bridge of her nose. She had fallen face down and her black hair draggled in blood. The slug, which was still in her head, evidently was from a small-caliber revolver or pistol; the assistant medical examiner guessed a .25. "A woman's gun," one of the precinct detectives told Bill Weigand, turning it over to him. "You wanted her," the precinct man said. "You've got her."

He hadn't, Bill said mildly, wanted her this way. He had wanted her talking.

"Well," the precinct man said, reasonably, "somebody else didn't. Huh?"

Bill agreed that it looked that way.

"The woman who got the Gipson dame," the precinct man said, as if stating a fact.

Bill agreed again, still mildly, but made a correction. "Whoever got the Gipson dame," he said. The precinct man said he thought it was a woman who got the Gipson dame. He said he thought everybody figured it that way.

"Right," Weigand said. "It figures that way. What about time? On this one?"

It had been recent—within two or three hours. Bill Weigand looked at his watch and said it was three-fifty. The precinct man looked at his watch and said yeah, it was.

"Not much before one, then," Bill said to the assist-ant medical examiner, who was standing, looking down at the body. "Not much after—not much after what, Doctor?"

The doctor turned around and looked at him.

"Well," he said, "I'd say she's been dead an hour, at the shortest."

"Between twelve-thirty and ten minutes of three, then?" Bill said.

The doctor said he guessed so. He said it was probably between one and two-thirty. He went toward the door. He told them to send it along any time. He paused, looked back, and said he hated to see them get it so young.

"Right," Bill said. "So do I. Or any time."

"Sure," the doctor said. "Abstractly." He went out. The man who was taking fingerprints dropped one dead hand on the floor and stepped over the body so he could reach the other hand. He began to make impres-sions from it on slips of paper. Weigand watched him a moment; watched the other fingerprint man, who was dusting doorknobs, the ironwork of the bed near which the girl had fallen, the sides and back of the wooden chair, the woodwork around the doors. Bill said he was probably finding plenty. The fingerprint man looked at him and twisted his mouth and nodded. He said it didn't look as if anybody had ever wiped anything in the room. He said the freshest were the girl's, if that mattered.

"On the outside knob?" Bill wanted to know.

The man shook his head. He said somebody had recently used a cloth to turn it, and blurred the prints. He said he hadn't got anything clear off it, even the girl's. Weigand was not pleased, but he was not sur-prised.

He talked to the elderly clerk on duty at the desk and the man answered him hurriedly, with something like fear in his eyes. The hotel in West Forty-second Street was familiar with the police, and familiarity had bred trepidation. Now the clerk was eager to tell what he knew. But he knew little. He was sure that Florence

Adams had gone out of the hotel a little after eleven. He had not seen her come back.

"But I guess she got back, all right," the man said.

"Right," Weigand said. "She got back."

The clerk said she must have got by without his seeing her. He said it could be.

"It ain't that we don't try to keep track of 'em, captain," he said. "You see how it is."

Weigand saw how it was. The lobby was small, but even so the clerk's counter was placed so that a man behind it might easily not see who came in and went out.

"And nobody asked for her?" Bill said. He said it without optimism, anticipating the shake of the clerk's head. Nobody had come to the desk and asked the room number of Miss Florence Adams. Nobody would have, planning to kill her. The girl must have given her murderer the number of her room. Or the murderer must have come in with her.

"Strangers?" Weigand asked. The man shook his head again.

"You know how it is, captain," he said. "Most of 'em is strangers. Except the ones who live here."

Bill Weigand said he knew how it was.

"And you didn't hear the shot?" he said. He was going over ground the precinct men had gone over.

"Not to know it was a shot," the man said. "I musta heard it, captain, but I musta thought it was a backfire."

"Or somewhere else and none of your business," Weigand said. The man shook his head, and the dirty white hair fluttered around its central baldness.

"Honest to God, captain," he said. "I didn't hear nothing I thought was a shot."

Whether he had or not, he was going to stick to a safer version. If he was getting away with something, he figured to get away with it. They were, for the time being, going to have to be content with the time interval they had. Twelve-thirty to two-fifty maximum; one and two-thirty minimum. It would do; so far as

Bill Weigand could see, it was going to have to do. So the next thing was: Where was everybody? It was something that you always got down to. Who had opportunity?

Men came through the lobby carrying a basket. The clerk looked at it; he had seen it before.

"Yeah," he said. "Curtains."

Then he looked at his own hands. He moved his fingers, carefully, with intention; testing their sentience. And then, oddly, almost gloatingly, he smiled.

Bill Weigand did not go back to the room. He went down to the police car in which he had told Pam North she could sit. There had been no need for either of them to assure the other that she was not going up to the room in which Florence Adams lay with her black hair in blood. Bill told Pam, briefly, what he had found.

"They won't come to us," he said. "They think they're being so damned bright—so damned bright."

Pam nodded, not saying anything. Her eyes were sober; she seemed to be looking at someone or something far away. She was silent as the police car turned downtown. She nodded when Bill said he would drop her anywhere she liked, and then she said, "The apartment, I guess, Bill."

"Probably," Bill said, and Pam knew he was thinking aloud, "she let somebody borrow her key—somebody who told her a good story and paid her a hundred dollars."

Pam's eyes came back, and they were enquiring.

"In her purse," he said." "A hundred dollars in tens and a little bit more. I should think that's where she got the hundred. But she read in the *News* that Miss Gipson had been murdered and got scared about her part in it. She went to the hotel, figuring we wouldn't find her. As we didn't—in time. Then she tried a shakedown."

"Or," Pam said, "wanted an explanation."

"Or both," Bill Weigand said. "She must have got some sort of explanation, anyhow. Somebody strung her along until he could get her and kill her."

"He?" Pam said, "I thought it was a woman, because you know why."

"She," Bill said. "He or she. It was a little gun, anyway."

"And?" Pam said.

"There was no perfume in the room," Bill said. "Oh—the body smelled of something. Not the right thing. The room—well, the room smelled of cordite. And blood."

Pam was silent until the car stopped outside the apartment house in which the Norths lived. Then, instead of getting out immediately, she sat a moment.

"Mrs. Burt had just come in," she said. "Hadn't she? Helen Burt? The maid thought she was out."

Or, Bill pointed out, could have been giving them the usual stall. Pam shook her head at that; she said it didn't sound like the usual stall.

"I think she had just come in," she said. "So—"

"So she could have been at the hotel," Bill finished for her. "Yes. I thought the maid didn't know, too. She could have been at the hotel. She could have been anywhere. And her husband had just come in, too. And so had, I suppose, several thousand other people in New York."

"I know," Pam said. "It just isn't impossible."

Obviously, Bill Weigand agreed, it wasn't impossible. Obviously Mrs. Burt's movements were interesting. So were the movements, he pointed out, of several other people—of John Gipson, Nora Frost, of Philip Spencer; of, for all they knew, a dozen other people whose names they didn't know.

Pam got out and Bill Weigand got out with her and got back in.

"Of course," Pam said, through the window, "it could have been one of the writers. Alexander Hill or Mrs. Abernathy or Mr. Robinson or even the Munroes. Although I don't think the Munroes, because they're married."

Bill Weigand looked at her, and his eyes widened.

"For God's sake why?" he said.

"She saw them," Pam told him. "Since she came

here. She had contact with them. It might be anybody she had had contact with."

"Including," Bill said, "the doorman at the Annex? The clerk? The waitress at whatever tea shop she went to? The Library attendants? The—"

"Oh yes," Pam said. "Of course, I said 'might.' "

Bill Weigand was thankful for that, and said so. He still looked puzzled.

"Why not the Munroes?" he said.

"They collaborate," Pam told him. "People don't, on murder. Not when they're married. Jerry and I wouldn't."

It seemed a little inconclusive, Bill told her. But for what it was worth, he thought it probably wasn't the Munroes.

"Or any of the others," he said. "People who write about murder don't murder."

If anything was inconclusive, Pam told him as the car started, that last was.

Mullins was waiting for Weigand at the office. Mullins looked, Bill Weigand decided as soon as he saw him, as if he had something.

"Well," Bill said, "did Backley tell you who did it, sergeant?"

Mullins was not dashed, which meant that he was more than usually confident.

"Maybe he did, loot," Mullins said. "It could just be he did."

Mullins had seen the attorney who handled the Gipson estate and who was most familiar with its ramifications. He had found nothing new there; he had retraced the ground Stein had covered efficiently. But, because Backley knew both John Gipson and Nora Frost, who had been Nora Gipson, Mullins had been able to go farther. He had, for one thing, given Backley the gist of the letter Nora had written her aunt the day before Amelia Gipson died.

Backley had looked grave. He was a smallish man with a resonant voice and a face built for proper gravity. He made deprecatory sounds with his tongue and lips. He shook his head. He said that it was an extremely unwise letter to have written.

"Particularly," Mullins said, "to a dame that's going to get killed."

The circumstances, Backley had agreed, made the letter particularly unfortunate. "But we must bear in mind that Mrs. Frost had no intimation that her aunt was to—die," he told Mullins.

Mullins remained silent.

"I sat that one out," he told Weigand, reporting. "He looked at me kinda funny and wanted to know did I think she did. I said we had no reason for thinking anything at this stage of the investigation. Right?"

"Right," Bill Weigand agreed. He smiled faintly to himself.

Backley had, judicially, recognized that he had no right to insist on a more definite answer. He had said that he, obviously, would regard any such suggestion as preposterous. To that Mullens had said merely, "Sure," dismissing it. He had asked whether Nora Frost—Major and Mrs. Frost—needed money.

On that point, Mr. Backley had been confident and assured. He had hoped that Mullins—he had hoped that he himself—would never need money more than the Frosts did at that moment. Kennet Frost, to begin with, had a very substantial income. Very substantial. Nora Frost, in the second place, had found her share of the income from the estate more than ample. She had had—the Frosts had had—no reason whatever for not wishing Amelia Gipson a long life; no reason whatever for wishing to accelerate the distribution of the trust established by Alfred Gipson. Whatever the letter referred to—and Mr. Backley was frank, he was almost eager, to say he didn't know—it did not refer to money. At any rate, it did not refer to the estate.

"I never thought it did," Weigand said. "It doesn't sound like a letter about money. It sounds like a letter about the emotions."

"O.K., loot," Mullins said. "There was no harm in asking him."

Clearly, Weigand agreed, they had to ask him.

"Then," Mullins said, "we went on to John—the nephew, John is."

"I can keep them straight," Weigand promised him.

"The nephew," Mullins repeated, keeping it straight anyway. "The chemist. Seems he was working on something top secret for the government at a laboratory up in Connecticut. I think it was something about atoms and—"

"Everybody now thinks all research is about the atoms," Weigand told him. "However—maybe it is."

Backley had said that much, said that John Gipson was well enough paid and engrossed in his work and had been willing to let it stop there. Mullins had also been ready to let it stop; it had been chance, more than anything, which had led to another question.

"Just sorta to fill in," Mullins said. "I asked him if Gipson was doing anything else. I didn't see why he should be."

Mr. Backley had looked even more judicial and had put the tips of his fingers together and regarded them, evidently seeking guidance. He apparently had found it.

The fact was, he had told Mullins, that John Gipson was also, in his spare time, conducting experiments of his own. Not on atoms. On plastics, Mr. Backley understood. He did not understand much else, except that John Gipson felt he had hit on something. With the war over, he expected to be released from government service. He wanted to go on with whatever he had on plastics. Mullins had got it, then.

"He wanted capital," Mullins had said, flatly. "This was the time to get into whatever the racket was, with things picking up. He didn't want to wait until—how long would he have had to wait?"

Backley had made further deprecating sounds with tongue and lips over that; he had looked grave and disapproving. But he had said that the money would be divided, as he had already told Mullins, when Nora was twenty-five. And Nora was now twenty-three.

"Two years might make the hell of a lot of difference

if young Gipson was onto something." Mullins said.

Backley had said he feared Sergeant Mullins was inclined to jump to conclusions. He said he did not know, actually, that Gipson was onto anything.

"But he thinks he is," Mullins said. "Don't he?"

Backley thought that over, and nodded.

"And he wants capital?"

Backley nodded again.

"And he don't want to let outsiders in by sharing whatever he's got," Mullins had guessed.

Backley did not nod this time. He looked very disapproving. He said that he had no information on that point. But he did not enter a denial.

Mullins had guessed then that Gipson had gone to his aunt, asking for his share—or a large part of his share—in advance. And had been refused. Was that it?

Backley stopped talking then. He said that he felt they were now in the realm of matters confidential between lawyer and client.

"Which is as good as an answer, ain't it?" Mullins wanted to know. There was triumph in the question.

Bill Weigand nodded slowly. It was as good as an answer. A denial would have violated no confidence. Only if Mullins had hit on the truth, or part of the truth, would there be reason for Mr. Backley's recourse to legal ethics.

So—John Gipson had a motive. He might believe— he might be right in believing—that his aunt was standing between him and real money—real money in the realest sense; the kind of money for which many men would do strange things, and had.

And John's sister, Nora, had written a strange letter.

It was time to talk to these young people. He knew enough now. It was high time. He looked at his watch. If O'Connor had caught them at the airport when they met the major, who had been due in at one o'clock, he had had plenty of time to report in. And he would have arranged an interview, which was what he was there for—or partly what he was there for. Weigand took a sheaf of papers out of his "In" basket and looked through them. O'Connor had reported, all right. He had reported that neither John Gipson nor his sister had appeared at the airport, and that no Major Frost—no major of any name—had got off the plane. The nearest O'Connor had come was a colonel, who was a regular, worked in Washington, and was named Jones. It was not very near.

A tall young man with blue eyes and wings on the left breast of his tunic looked at Bill Weigand and said, "Yes?" His tone reserved decision.

"Major Frost?" Bill said.

The young man agreed he was Major Frost. Bill Weigand identified himself.

"Oh," Major Frost said, "about Nora's aunt."

"Right," Weigand said. "Mrs. Frost was coming to see us. Or I thought she was. There was a misunderstanding, apparently. So I came to see her."

"Come ahead," Major Kennet Frost said. "We were just having a drink. You can have one with us."

He turned and went back into the apartment, assuming Weigand would follow him. It was an apartment with a sunken living room and there were two steps down from the tiny foyer. There was an ornamental iron railing part around the little platform onto which you entered, Bill Weigand followed the young major of the Air Force down into the living room.

"This is that detective, Nora," Kennet Frost said. "Weigand. Lieutenant Weigand."

Nora Frost was slender and very lovely, with soft brown hair which seemed to flow around her face. She had large brown eyes and she widened them slightly at Bill Weigand. She said, "Oh." She said, "Oh, *dear*."

"We expected to find you at the airport," Bill said. "Meeting the major. The boys must have misunderstood."

"Oh," she said. "You went there? Please sit down, lieutenant."

Major Frost sat down on the sofa by his wife. Weigand sat in a deep chair, more or less facing them.

"Scotch?" the major said. "I've got some scotch. Understand it's been hard for you people to get."

His tone tacitly, inoffensively, opened a gulf between Weigand and himself—Weigand suspected it opened a gulf between the Army Air Force and all other persons everywhere. Particularly all civilians. It was a gulf which would shrink, Weigand thought. He hazarded a guess.

"You're being released, major?" he said, pleasantly. Major Frost frowned momentarily. He was hardly older than his wife, Weigand thought. Twenty-five at most would do it. He had been very confident, very assured, very expert, but that was in another world. It was tough on kids, Bill thought. But the insistence of the Police Department that he remain civilian had been tough on him, so it evened up, in a way. He looked at the ribbons on the major's tunic. One of them was the ribbon of the Distinguished Flying Cross. The major had been very good, in that other world.

"Terminal leave," Major Frost said. He smiled, suddenly. "I'll have trouble with scotch too, I suppose. By the way, it was merely that I got on an earlier airplane."

"And telephoned me from the airport," Nora Frost said, quickly. "So John and I didn't go out. I met Ken for lunch and of course I should have called your office, lieutenant, but—"

"We were busy," Frost said. "I'd been out there twenty-four months. And anyway, I don't know what she can tell you, lieutenant."

"Neither do I," Weigand said. He picked up the scotch and soda his nod had accepted. "We have to—explore all possibilities, you know."

"I hadn't seen Amelia for days," Nora said. She spoke quickly, almost hurriedly. She took up her glass and finished the pale drink that remained in it. She held it up and Kennet Frost took it and went to a table which held a silver tray and bottles. He made her a fresh drink and brought it back.

"I can't believe anybody would have wanted to kill her," Nora said. "Why should they?"

That was one of the things he was trying to find out,

Bill said. Meanwhile, Mrs. Frost would have to believe that somebody had killed her. Somebody had substituted sodium fluoride for one of the powders she apparently was in the habit of taking.

"Dr. Powers' Medicine," Nora Frost said. "She'd taken it for years. She used to take boxes of it up to Maine when we went there in the summer. You remember, Ken?"

"Yeah," Kennet Frost said. "Anyway, I remember your telling me about it. You said she was always dosing herself."

He was a polite young man, and had been to the right places. So there was not quite contempt in his tone. But people who dosed themselves were a long way from his circle.

Weigand said he supposed that many people knew of Amelia Gipson's habit, and Nora Frost said everybody who knew her, she should think. She sipped her drink. She stretched lovely legs out in front of her and looked at them.

"Don't think I'm not sorry about it," she said, still looking at her legs. "I am sorry. Amelia was—she was somebody I'd known all my life. She was—family."

"You were fond of her?" Weigand wanted to know.

She looked at him.

"Not particularly," she said. "Except—because she was family. She more or less brought me up." She smiled faintly. "As I've no doubt you know," she said. "I never thought much about her until recently, I suppose. As—as a person. She was just Aunt Amelia, who brought me up, and who spent summers with me up in Maine while Ken was gone."

She stopped, because Kennet Frost was looking at her. It was a look Weigand had no trouble interpreting. Major Frost thought his pretty wife was talking too much.

"All right, major," Bill said. He spoke lightly, easily. "Mrs. Frost's attitude is quite understandable." He paused and his smile faded. "Miss Gipson was poisoned," he said. "Somebody wanted to kill her and did. This wasn't a result of—a lack of particular fondness, as Mrs. Frost puts it. She was killed because somebody thought it was necessary, for his own purposes, that she be out of the way."

"You asked if she was fond of her aunt," Frost reminded him. His tone was suspicious. He would fight for Nora, and he had proved to be a good fighter. In that other world. It was interesting that he thought she might need fighting for.

He was merely, Weigand said, trying to find out how well Mrs. Frost had known her aunt. It was useful, he said, to find out as much about eople who had been murdered as could be found out. The way to do that was to talk to people who had known them well.

"Character enters into murder," Weigand said. "The character of the victim, as well as the character of the killer."

"It's all right, Ken," Nora Frost said. "The lieutenant knows I didn't kill Amelia."

Weigand shook his head at that, but a smile tempered the implication. He said that, abstractly, he didn't know that anyone had not killed Amelia Gipson. He would not know that, he pointed out, until he knew who had killed her.

"Well," Frost said, "Nora didn't. I didn't."

"By the way," Weigand said, "speaking of you, major. Just how much earlier was this earlier plane you caught?"

"Four hours," Frost said. He looked hard at Weigand. "I wasn't here yesterday afternoon, if that's what you're getting at," he said. "I was in Kansas City, arguing about a priority with some civilian." He paused and seemed, somehow, to be looking at himself. "Hell," he said, and there was surprise in his tone, "I'm next thing to a civilian myself." It seemed to astonish him.

"And you telephoned your wife from LaGuardia?" Weigand said. "When was that?"

"About ten," Frost said. "I told her not to come out. I came here and we went out to lunch. We got back about three and have been here since. Why?"

Weigand told him why. He told him succinctly.

"I never heard of the girl," Frost said. "It seems like a tough break. But I never heard of her."

"Mrs. Frost?" Weigand said.

She shook her head, her softly curled brown hair floating about it. She had never heard of Florence Adams. Her face reflected a kind of concern. She said it was too bad about the girl. She sounded as if she thought it too bad about the girl.

"Where did you lunch?" Weigand said. He saw hardness in Frost's face.

"Major," he said, "I'm doing a job that has to be done. I'm a policeman, looking for a murderer. I never saw you and Mrs. Frost before in my life, or heard of you. I don't know whether you are the most truthful people in the world, or whether you're liars. All I know—*know*, major—is that you are wearing an Army uniform with wings and ribbons and a major's leaves."

The major looked annoyed. Then he smiled suddenly.

"Want to see my I.D. card, lieutenant?" he said.

"Yes," Weigand said. He looked at it. When he returned it, his own badge was cupped in his hand. He let them both look at it.

"All right," Frost said, "we're both who we say we are, apparently. We had lunch at Twenty-one."

"Did you see anyone you knew?" Weigand asked.

Frost smiled, but his wife answered.

"I'm afraid we only saw each other, lieutenant," she said. Her voice was soft.

"And would rather now," Weigand agreed.

Frost nodded. There was emphasis in his nod. He was, Weigand thought, alternately mature and very young.

"We don't have to hurry," Nora Frost said, and her voice was soft. She was speaking, Weigand thought, to her husband rather than to him. "Not any more."

Kennet Frost smiled at her. Weigand thought they were very much in love, and had already waited a good while. Frost brought himself back, sharply, youthfully. He was very matter of fact, suddenly.

"Obviously," he said, "Nora inherits money now

that her aunt is dead. You know that, I suppose?"

"Oh yes," Weigand said. "Naturally."

"And you think it's a possible motive?" Frost said. He was still matter-of-fact.

Bill said that money was always a possible motive. Particularly a good deal of money; particularly if somebody needed money.

"We don't," Frost said. "You can check on that."

"Right," Bill Weigand said. "So we can."

"Why don't you?" Frost wanted to know. "Then if you find out we are broke and have to have Nora's money so badly we can't wait a couple of years, and find out that I was really in New York yesterday and not in Kansas City, come back?"

"Yes," Weigand said, "if I find out those things, I'll come back. Meanwhile, there's a point I want to clear up with your wife, major."

"Well," Frost said, "clear it up."

Weigand hesitated a moment. He wished Major Frost would go out and buy a package of cigarettes. He obstructed. But Weigand doubted that Frost would go.

"Right," he said. He turned to Nora Frost, his movement excluding her husband. "You wrote a letter to your aunt the day before she died, Mrs. Frost. It seemed to us an odd letter, under the circumstances. Do you remember it?"

The girl's eyes seemed to flicker for a second. She picked up her glass and she was stalling for time. The glass trembled slightly in her hands and, although she raised it to her lips, Weigand did not see her swallow. He had seen that happen before; a glass can clink against teeth if the hand holding it trembles.

The girl waited too long, and then, knowing it had been too long, spoke too quickly.

"Yes," she said. "I remember it."

"You will understand, then, why we want an explanation," Weigand said. His voice was no longer casual.

"That's why you came, isn't it?" Nora said.

"Wait a minute!" Frost said.

Weigand turned to him.

"You're not in this, major," he said. "Unless you also know about the letter. Do you?"

"I don't know what you're talking about," Frost said. "But you can't—"

"Your wife wrote her aunt a letter which requires explanation," Weigand said. "I expect to get that explanation. Don't think I can't, major. If you interfere, I shall have to take Mrs. Frost somewhere else to get the explanation. If it's a simple one, I'd rather not. But you can have it either way."

The major looked at Weigand for a moment. He looked puzzled.

"Hell," he said, "you talk like the colonel."

Weigand did not smile. He said, "Well, major?"

"I'm sorry, sir," Major Frost said. "If anything needs explaining, I know Nora can explain it."

"Right," Weigand said. "I have a copy of the letter here, Mrs. Frost. Do you want me to read it?"

The girl spoke very quickly. She spoke almost as if she were frightened.

"No!" she said. "Oh no, please!"

Then, involuntarily, she looked at her husband and looked away again. Weigand's eyes followed hers. The young face of Major Frost was very young—and very puzzled.

"Look," Frost said, and his voice was puzzled, too. He held out his hand, tentatively, as if for the letter. "Let me—"

"No," Nora said. "Please, Ken. I don't want you to."

Bill Weigand was glad he had not insisted on having Frost go out for cigarettes. He was very glad.

"Well, Mrs. Frost?" he said. "What is the explanation?"

The girl hesitated. It was obvious she was trying to work out a story. It was pathetically obvious. It was also obvious that she had not expected this, and had no story ready. Which might mean that she was innocent. Or might merely mean she underestimated the police.

"I. . . ." she said. "It wasn't anything important."

Weigand shook his head.

"It had to be important, Mrs. Frost," he said. "You can't remember the letter. You said something that your aunt was going to do was . . ." he referred to the letter . . . " 'wicked and barbaric, no better than murder.' It had to be important."

The girl shook her head. But there was no assurance in the gesture.

"I was excited," she said. "I . . . I thought . . . she was trying to . . . to come between Ken and me."

Weigand waited, but she did not continue. He thought she could not continue. She was clearly frightened now, and no longer hopeful of hiding it. Her slender hands were working together. He looked at Frost and saw bewilderment—and more than bewilderment—in his face. Frost, he would guess, was entirely surprised by this, because he was entirely new to this.

"How?" Weigand pressed her. "What had she found out? You wrote that—?"

"I know!" the girl said. "I know what I wrote! I told you not to read the letter!"

"Then tell me what it means, Mrs. Frost," Weigand said. "Tell me what she had found out; what she was doing—what made you threaten her, Mrs. Frost."

"I—" the girl started. Then she turned to her husband, and all her face asked for his help.

"You don't need to explain anything, darling," Frost said. His voice was low and steady—and it was surprisingly gentle. "You don't need to explain anything. Nobody can make you."

Weigand waited.

"Nobody can make you, Nora," Frost repeated. "I know it was all right—I—I know it was all right. Whatever it was." He turned to Weigand. "You can't force her to explain anything, lieutenant," he said.

Weigand shrugged slightly.

"Obviously," he said. His voice was cold and entirely without emphasis. "But I can make her wish she had, major. If there is an innocent explanation, she'd better give it." He paused, and now he spoke directly to Mrs. Frost. "Even if it is embarrassing," he said.

"It isn't—" the girl began, and then the doorbell rang. Bill Weigand did not say anything, but he could hardly have been annoyed more.

Major Frost clearly was not annoyed. He went quickly across the living room and up the two steps to the entrance balcony. He said, "Hello, John," with what sounded like real pleasure.

"Is Nora here?" another male voice said—a lighter, quicker voice than the major's. "Backley just called and the police—"

Frost picked it up quickly.

"Somebody from the police is here, John," he said. "Lieutenant Weigand. He's been asking Nora a few questions."

John Gipson was in by that time. He stopped and looked down into the living room. He was a slim man, slighter than his brother-in-law, quicker in movement. You could have guessed relationship between him and the girl on the sofa. Their hair was of the same brown and their brown eyes were similarly set. And as John looked across at his sister, he smiled quickly, and there was warmth as well as enquiry in his smile. He turned to Weigand and did not smile.

"I suppose you think we were in a hurry for the money," John Gipson said. His tone hinted that that was the obvious thing for a policeman to think; that, being obvious, it could not be true.

"I don't know," Weigand said. "You're John Gipson? The nephew? I did hear you were in a hurry for the money, as a matter of fact."

"Backley talks too much," Gipson said. "Have you been badgering Nora?"

"I've been asking her questions," Bill Weigand said, mildly. "If they badgered her I suppose it was because they were hard questions to answer. You were in a hurry for the money? You wanted it to develop a new process you've discovered?"

"Backley's an old fool," Gipson said. He spoke chiefly to his sister. "I always said he was an old fool."

"Backley is sworn to uphold the law and assist the police," Weigand told him. "He's an officer of the court. Did you want money in a hurry?"

"Not that much of a hurry," Gipson said. He did not, Weigand thought, seem alarmed. "Anyway, I wouldn't kill Amelia. Hell, we've known her all our lives."

Weigand told him that that was hardly proof.

"However," he said, "I haven't suggested that you killed your aunt. When did you see her last?"

"Days ago," Gipson said. He crossed over to the table and mixed himself a drink. He looked at his sister's glass and saw it was half full. Then he looked at Frost's glass.

"Pour you some of your liquor, Ken?" he said. Kennet Frost nodded, and Gipson crossed to the sofa, picked up Frost's glass, poured scotch into it and put in soda and brought it back. "Days ago," he said. "However, I talked to her on the telephone yesterday. Asked her if she wouldn't change her mind and come through with my share. She wouldn't. Seemed perfectly natural; perfectly in character. I didn't think she would."

"Why wouldn't she?" Weigand said. "Didn't she believe in your discovery? Invention? Whatever it is?"

"A new process," Gipson said. "Having to do with plastics. Do you want to hear details?"

His voice implied that Weigand would not understand them if he did. Weigand shook his head. He said he did not want to hear them. He said if they became important in any connection, Gipson could explain them to somebody in the department who would understand.

"Of whom," he said, "there are several, Mr. Gipson."

"Are there?" Gipson said. "As to Amelia—I don't know what she believed. All I know is she wouldn't give me the money."

"Which," Weigand said, "probably annoyed you."

John Gipson drank and said Weigand was damn right it did.

"Whereupon," he said, "I brought her some nice fresh poison and said, 'Drink this, will you, auntie?' and she said, 'Of course, dear boy. Anything for a nephew,' and there we were."

"Do you think it's funny, Mr. Gipson?" Weigand said. "It wasn't, you know. It wasn't at all funny."

Gipson looked at Weigand, and Weigand's expression did not encourage light-heartedness.

"No," Gipson said, "I didn't think it's funny, lieutenant. Amelia wasn't a dream aunt in all respects, but I'd like to see you get the guy who killed her. Very much." He paused and examined Weigand's face. "I didn't kill her, if you really think I did," he said. "I don't know who did, except that it wasn't Nora and it wasn't Ken and it wasn't me."

"All right," Weigand said, equably. "Where were you today from noon until two o'clock—at about the time you were supposed to be meeting the major at the airport?"

John Gipson looked at the major, surprised.

"He got in on an earlier—" he began.

"I know," Weigand said, "I understand why you weren't at the airport. Where were you?"

"Why?" Gipson said.

Briefly, Weigand told him why.

"That was a damned dirty trick," Gipson said. "Rope the girl in, and then kill her because you had. Did he take back the hundred, too?"

Bill Weigand shook his head. He waited.

"I was having lunch most of the time, I guess," Gipson said. "By myself, not wanting to horn in on these two. Then I went downtown to see a man." He looked at Weigand. "Still hush-hush, that is," he said. "But it was about two-thirty that I got there, so it wouldn't help anyway. No alibi."

He waited, as if for a comment, but Weigand made none. Instead he asked, for the record, whether any of them knew any reason why somebody—not one of

them—might have wanted to poison Amelia Gipson.
The girl shook her head and Major Frost merely
looked at Bill Weigand.

"She was a difficult person," John Gipson said, after
a moment. He spoke slowly. "She was very—
righteous. She wanted other people to behave as—in
accordance with her standards. Few people did. When
they didn't, Amelia thought it was her duty to make
trouble for them. I've heard she made trouble for
several people. At the college, chiefly. But I don't
know any details." He looked at Weigand. "What I'm
trying to say is that she wasn't an unlikely candidate
for what she got," he said. "She might have stepped
on somebody too hard. That's all I can think of."

Bill Weigand nodded. Then he turned to the girl
again.

"I still want to hear about the letter, you know," he
said.

She had been nervous, and Bill Weigand had seen
her nervousness and waited. She had dreaded it and
now it had come. And now she turned to her brother
and her eyes sought his help.

"Letter?" Gipson said. "What—" Then he broke
off. His eyes questioned Nora Frost and she nodded.
There was concern in his mobil face—quick concern.

"A letter my sister wrote to Amelia?" he said. It had
the form of a question, but it was hardly a question.

"You knew about it, I gather," Bill said. "Yes—that
letter. Your sister doesn't seem to want to explain it."

"I know about it," Gipson said. "It had nothing to
do with any of this. It was private."

Dryly, Weigand said he had gathered it was private.
But nothing, he said, was private in a murder investigation.

"However," he said, "if it doesn't mean anything, if
it really hasn't anything to do with this, it can stop with
me."

Brother and sister conferred, without speech. Major
Frost looked at his wife and then at Gipson, and his
eyes were puzzled and unhappy. Whatever it was, Bill

Weigand thought, he's not in on it; it's something they're keeping from him. In which case—

"However," he said, "I can't force it from you, as you pointed out earlier, major. I'd advise you to change your mind, Mrs. Frost. If you do, you can telephone me. But I'd change my mind before tomorrow, if I were you." He paused to let it register. "Talk to your brother, Mrs. Frost," he said, then. "I'm sure he'll advise you to get in touch with me."

He stood up, then. He looked down at them.

"Of course you know it's only begun," he said. "Murder cases don't stop." He took a step toward the door and Major Frost arose and went ahead of him. "Not until they're finished," Weigand added. He turned, then, and went out the door Frost had opened. He would have liked to hear what the three said to one another when the door closed, but that was impracticable. He thought he would pick up the gist of it as time went on.

9

Jerry North opened the apartment-house door and said, "Hey, Pam," which was a way of indicating that he was not alone and that Pam North should bear that in mind when greeting him. It was not always certain precisely what Pam would say by way of greeting when she thought he was alone. This time, however, she spoke from the living room.

"It's come," she said. "And it's the smallest—"

She came out into the foyer and said, "Oh, hello Mr. Hill."

Alexander Hill said, "Good evening, Mrs. North."

"What came?" Jerry said.

Pam looked at him wide-eyed and asked if he couldn't see it. He looked at her more carefully. A tiny animal was perched on her right shoulder. It looked at him through bright blue eyes, with bright interest. It said "yow!" It kept on saying "yow!", not in displeasure, so far as Jerry could see, but merely to show interest, awareness and presence. It had a tiny face which at first looked dirty and the rest of it was a brownish white. Not all of it was visible as it regarded them from Pam North's shoulder.

"I think," Pam said, "that it looks like a very tiny polar bear. What do you think, Jerry?"

"I think," Jerry said, "that it looks like a very tiny Siamese cat."

Pam looked at him and seemed disappointed.

116

"Oh, that," Pam said. "Of course it looks like a very tiny Siamese cat. It *is* a very tiny Siamese cat. But I think it looks even more like a very tiny polar bear."

Jerry picked the little cat off Pam's shoulder. It began to purr instantly on being touched; there was a great deal of purr for so very little cat.

"Of course," Jerry said, "it also looks a little like a monkey."

He held it in one hand. It climbed up his arm, hurriedly, as if it had just remembered an appointment. It sat on his shoulder. It bit his ear—gently, on the whole.

"And it acts rather like a monkey," Jerry said.

"Polar bears can climb," Pam pointed out and thought a moment. "Or can't they? Do they just sit on cakes of ice? Do you know, Mr. Hill?"

"What?" said Mr. Hill, who was looking with surprise at the cat. The cat looked in surprise at Mr. Hill, who wore a black beard. He was a small man, rather slight, and the beard was dominant.

"Polar bears," Mrs. North prompted. "Cakes of ice."

"So far as I know," Mr. Hill said, "all bears climb. Is it a new cat?"

"It just came," Pam said. "Of course it won't take the place of—"

"But it will," Jerry said quickly. "I mean, of course it won't be the same. But it will be something else—something different—in approximately the same place."

"All right," Pam said. "I know that's true. But she does remind me of Ruffy, because she's a cat. I suppose that's why I keep thinking of her as a very small polar bear."

Jerry blinked slightly and looked, involuntarily, at Alexander Hill. Hill, he thought, was looking a little dazed. Jerry was familiar with the look; he had worn it.

"I think," Pam said, "that we ought to call her Martini. Then we can call her Teeny for short and she'll come to either, because after all it's the vowels."

"What?" Mr. Hill said, in a somewhat strained voice.

"They answer to vowel sounds," Jerry explained. "They don't really seem to hear the rest. When we had Pete he would come just as quickly if we merely said 'Eeee.' If he wanted to, naturally."

Mr. Hill looked at Gerald North with a somewhat fixed expression.

"Perhaps," he said, "I had better come back some other time and look over the Gipson notes. Only I'm anxious to get on with it, you know. But, I mean to say . . . at such a moment. . . ."

"Oh," Pam said, "we just bought her. It's not a moment, particularly. Except, of course, we're interested. What do you think of the name, Jerry. Because look at her tail."

Jerry looked at her tail. It was very straight and, at the moment, Martini was wearing it straight up. It bristled somewhat and looked like a spike on the end of the little cat.

"She wears it cocked," Pam said. "Cocktail. So Martini, naturally."

"Or Manhattan," Mr. Hill said. "Or even Stinger."

It was clear that he was getting into the spirit of the thing. But both of the Norths looked at him in honest surprise. Mrs. North, particularly, looked as if she could hardly believe her ears.

"Oh," she said, "you couldn't name her anything like that. Those. Not such a *nice* little cat."

"Oh," Mr. Hill said.

"Speaking of drinks," Jerry North said, "if you'll take Martini, Pam, I'll make them."

He plucked Martini off his shoulder and gave her back to Pam. Pam put her on the floor and she ran off.

"She runs like a rocking horse," Pam said. "It must be because her hind legs are longer than they ought to be and she doesn't understand it yet. Of course, they ought to be longer than they ought to be, because all Siamese's are."

Rather quickly, Jerry asked Alexander Hill what it

would be and, very quickly, Mr. Hill said rye and water, if it wasn't too much trouble. They went in the living room after the little cat. As they entered, it flattened itself on the carpet, and, with almost terrifying intensity, began to stalk toward them. It got close to Pam's feet, jumped straight up in the air and came down twisted a little sideways. The tiny tail also twisted with the tiny cat.

"All right, Teeny, I'm dead," Pam said. She picked the little cat up. Jerry went into the kitchen after bottles and began to come out with them.

"Mr. Hill is going to write the Gipson case," he said. "For the book. As well as the . . . ."

He went back again.

"As the first story in the book," Mr. Hill said, "Piquant, don't you think?"

"In the book Miss Gipson was doing reseach on?" Pam said. "The one you and the others are putting together—but of course."

"Piquant," Mr. Hill said. "Definitely." His expression changed slightly as he regarded his own thoughts. "Also a natural," he said. "It ought to make the book if we can work fast enough. Of course, it will be all the better if it isn't solved."

He seemed to wait for Pam North to say something. She said, "Why?" and decided that that was the proper thing for her to have said. Mr. Hill brightened and nodded, approvingly.

"Precisely," he said. *"Precisely.* Because there will be freedom of speculation. Added zest. Don't you think?"

Pam North said she saw what he meant.

"Only of course, Bill wants to solve it," she pointed out. "And, naturally, he's a friend of ours."

"It will be better for the book," Mr. Hill said, with finality. "Much better. And I have no expectation that it will be solved. None whatever."

"Haven't you?" Pam said.

"No," Mr. Hill said. "None whatever."

"Well," Pam said. "They usually are."

Jerry came back in with a tray and put it down on a

table. He poured rye into a jigger, looked at it and poured it into a glass. He put in ice.

"Are what?" he said. "Much water?"

"Very little, please," Mr. Hill said. "Solved, Mrs. North thinks. I was saying that I thought the Gipson case wouldn't be. And pointing out that we'll do better if it isn't."

Jerry nodded to that, gave Mr. Hill his drink, and began to mix martinis. But it would also, he pointed out, be better for the murderer.

"Oh," Mr. Hill said, "that." He dismissed it.

"What Mr. Hill wants to do," Jerry explained, emptying ice out of the cocktail glasses and filling them with very pale martinis, "is to look over the notes she made on the other cases."

"Precisely," Mr. Hill said. "Precisely. There is room for speculation, there. What unappreciated slip of what unknown murderer may Miss Gipson not have detected as she browsed among these almost forgotten records of yesterday's hatred, revenge and greed? What may she have seen, that had not been seen before, about the stammering Mr. Purdy, the dapper little doctor named Merton and his hoarded cultures of death, about the dim figure who, for reasons never guessed at, ended the life of the pretty girl from the Midwest who had come to New York with her only capital, beauty, and her days so mercilessly short?"

"I don't know," Pam said. "What?"

"What?" Mr. Hill said.

"Oh," Pam said, "I thought you were asking us."

Jerry looked at her and, almost imperceptibly, shook his head.

"Oh," Mr. Hill said. "I was just giving an idea. Something like that I think, don't you, North? If it isn't solved, of course." He paused and spoke slowly, almost as if to himself. "It will be disconcerting if it is solved," he said. "Very disconcerting."

"Of course," Pam told herself, "he's merely thinking about the success of the book. And the future of his own speculations."

But she looked at Jerry. Jerry sipped his cocktail and she thought he looked rather puzzled. But she could not catch his eyes.

"Pam has a theory," Jerry said, then. "Very interesting. Perhaps not impossible. She thinks it was Mrs. Willard Burt. The one who wrote the letter I mentioned."

Mr. Hill looked at Pam North with surprise and, it seemed to her, some incredulity.

"Why?" he said.

"Because she's really Helen Merton," Pam said. "Her name is Helen, you know. Suppose it was really she and not her husband who killed off her family. Was there any reason it couldn't have been?"

Mr. Hill looked at her thoughtfully.

"Not that I remember," he said. "Although I don't know that the point was ever raised. It's—ingenious."

"She's about the right age," Pam said. "She could have gone away somewhere after she divorced the doctor and come back—perhaps with another last name—and married Mr. Burt. And Amelia Gipson, who knew her before, may have put two and two together and realized that it was really she who had killed off her parents and brothers and sisters, for the money. And she may have threatened to expose her and given her a chance to explain. Which would be the reason for the letter Mrs. Burt wrote. And then Mrs. Burt killed her."

"It is ingenious," Mr. Hill told Gerald North. "Very ingenious. And not impossible. Precisely. Not impossible."

He looked thoughtfully at Mrs. North.

"What two and two did she put together?" he wanted to know.

Pam shook her head. She said that was the trouble. She said that obviously, it wasn't complete. She said, "Ouch!" Martini had run up Pam's stockinged leg. "Martini!" Pam said. "You hurt, baby." She picked the tiny cat up and put it in her lap. It climbed her and sat on her shoulder and began to talk, loudly, into her ear.

"I wish *you* stammered," she said, to the cat. "It might slow you down. Did he, really?"

"Mr. Purdy?" Mr. Hill said. "Oh yes. Quite badly, I understand. But he still found women with money to marry him."

"Did he?" Pam said. "More than one?"

So he understood, Mr. Hill told her. A friend of his who had investigated the case said that that was one of the things the police were looking into when Purdy was killed in the crash as he tried to get away. They thought there had been at least one other case which was too close a parallel to be mere coincidence.

"You mean," Pam said, "he did it professionally?"

Mr. Hill said that there had been reason to think that he had; that the police had thought he had.

"You'd think, then, that he'd have been more careful," Pam said. "More—professional." She shook her head. "It seems like a very difficult way to make a living," she said. "Marrying women with money and killing them off."

"It turned out to be," Jerry said. "They'd have caught him except for an accident."

Alexander Hill shook his head. He said they didn't understand. He said it was the excitement, the challenge.

"There wasn't a war when he was the right age," he said. "Or if there was—I suppose he could have been in the first one—he didn't get in it. This took the place. It was a dangerous way to live."

It turned out, Pam said, to be a way to die, but then she shook her head, correcting herself. Flying in a commercial airplane had proved the way to die, so far as Purdy was concerned.

"It might have been," Mr. Hill agreed. "That was part of it—part of the challenge. He put his mind against all the other minds; he played an elaborate game of wits with the rest of society. There was always danger in his life and danger is—" He broke off, and his eyes looked through Pam. "Men realized that once," he said. "The great excitement of life is the risk of losing life. Not as we all must some time—

dully. But facing a challenge—putting all your skill to work, trusting to all your luck, gambling. The same thing you get in a game, only a thousand times more intense. Not a cup at stake—or money—or your name in the newspapers. Life at stake. The strange, almost unbearable excitement of mortal combat."

He stopped and nodded to himself.

"Some soldiers know it," he said. "Along with the boredom. Flyers must have known it—their skill, their luck against death. Moments of indescribable brightness. Even terror must be a kind of brightness."

"I've been scared," Pam said. "It wasn't a kind of brightness." She remembered. "It was more a kind of darkness," she said.

Hill shook his head at her.

"Not for everybody," he said. "Obviously. Most of us want to be safe and sane. At most, to drive a car too fast—the obvious things. A little keying up does for most people. But there are some—I think Frank Purdy may have been one—for which the little things aren't enough. They want to play the most dangerous game of all—and murder, in our ordinary life, is the most dangerous game a man can play."

"However," Jerry North said, "I don't suppose he minded the money." Jerry spoke dryly.

Obviously, Alexander Hill said, the man had to live. He could not enjoy facing the sharp edge of danger if he were going hungry in old clothes.

"A certain—elegance—would be necessary," Mr. Hill said, with assurance. "Otherwise, how be debonair?"

"Look," Mrs. North said, "Have you any reason to think that Mr. Purdy felt any of these things? That he wanted to be debonair or live a dangerous life?" She shook her head. "After all," she pointed out, "he was named Purdy."

She was surprised that Mr. Hill nodded almost eagerly.

"Precisely," he said. "*Pre*cisely. An ordinary name; not a romantic name. Don't you see that that may very well have been it? That if he had been named—oh, memorably—he might never have felt the need for excitement? His whole life may have been a revulsion against a dull and ordinary name—a name without history, without association."

"No," Pam North said, "I can't say I do, Mr. Hill. Do you, really?"

"I. . . ." Hill began. The he stopped suddenly and his manner changed. "Forgive me," he said. "A literary fancy, obviously. Actually I suppose Purdy killed vulgarly for money. Another vulgar action in a vulgar world." He looked at Mrs. North and smiled. It was not, Pam North thought, a particularly friendly smile. "Common sense," he said. "You return me to actuality, Mrs. North. Of course, my speculation was far-fetched."

"I merely meant," Pam said, feeling that somehow she had failed one of Mr. Hill's better moments, "that Mr. Purdy sounds as if he had been a rather ordinary person. Only with peculiar habits."

"No doubt," Mr. Hill said. "No doubt. You will forgive an old romancer. It is—occupational." He looked at her and smiled again. "I assure you," he said, "that my feet are quite firmly on the ground. Quite firmly."

"Drink?" Jerry said.

Alexander Hill did not mind if he did. But he drank quickly; he said that this was very pleasant, but that there was work to be done. If he might have the notes? He wanted to read them that night; he wanted to write this macabre introduction to a book of crimes as soon as he could get about it. Jerry went to get the notes.

"Won't you have to wait to see how it comes out?" Pam asked Mr. Hill. "I mean—suppose you just get started and it's solved?"

Mr. Hill nodded. He said there was that. But he said that it did not matter greatly. The fact was there; the mood would grow from it. It was the mood that was important. How it came out was incidental.

"But," he said, "I shall write, I think, on the assumption that the case will not be solved. At least, not immediately. I shall, if it is at all possible, maintain the mood of mystery."

Pam merely nodded, and looked a little abstracted. Jerry came back with the notes, and Alexander Hill rose almost immediately. The cat jumped, after alarmed preparations, from Pam's lap and advanced on Mr. Hill's foot. Mr. Hill looked at it and moved his foot. He moved it rather quickly, because Martini had merely begun her stalk. She sat down, looked disappointed, and then turned suddenly and bit her tail. She paid no further attention to Mr. Hill and Mr. Hill went away.

"That's a very funny man," Pam said, after she had heard the elevator door close.

Jerry was pouring fresh drinks. He said there was no doubt that Mr. Hill was a very funny man.

"However," he said, "he writes a mean piece. Which is what we want. Drink up."

Pam drank up. Jerry refilled their glasses. The cat clambered up his trouser leg, its eyes round and blue and excited. It went out his arm, clinging, and smelled the drink in his glass. It drew back and said "yow!" It returned along his arm, holding tight, glancing down at the floor in what looked like trepidation. It reached his lap and began to purr.

"Now there," Pam said, "is somebody who does live dangerously. Martini. But you have to be a cat."

Jerry shook his head. He said that millions of men and women and children had been living dangerously—dreadfully too dangerously—for years.

"I mean in peace," Pam said. "In ordinary life."

What did she mean ordinary life, Jerry wanted to know. Because it was peace which was extraordinary, not war. Had been, always.

"Perhaps not now," Pam said. "Not any more. Perhaps now danger is too dangerous."

Jerry said he hoped so. He said that, in spite of everything, he had grown fond of the human race. He did not say it as if he meant to be humorous. Pam looked at him quickly. She got up quickly and went over and leaned down and kissed the back of his neck. Neither said anything, but Jerry looked up and smiled at her and began to stroke the tiny cat. Pam smiled back at him and went back to her chair.

"Speaking of Mr. Hill," she said. "Does he really believe all that? And is it true?"

Jerry shrugged. He said that he didn't know Hill well enough to be certain. He might. It was a literary fancy; Mr. Hill did not expect people to take him seriously. Which did not prove that he was not, really, serious.

"As to whether it's true," he said, "I don't know. I suppose there's truth in it."

"Did you ever feel that way?" Pam said.

Jerry shrugged. He said not very strongly. Not since he was much younger.

"But you wanted to get into it," Pam said. "I know you did."

That had been for other reasons, Jerry said. As she knew, he said.

"Altogether?" Pam said.

"Oh yes," Jerry said. "As far as I know."

"I think," Pam said, "that Mr. Hill really feels that way. He's very small, for a man. It might be—like Mr. Purdy's name. That could be why he wears a beard."

"To give distinction," Jerry said. "Yes, I've always supposed so. In his case. Not that he needs it."

Perhaps, Pamela North said, he wanted to be distinguished in some other way; perhaps he wanted to live some other way. Perhaps he—oh, wanted to fly an airplane in combat. Be a knight. Live dangerously.

"Perhaps," she said, "he was really talking about himself. Perhaps. . . ."

She stopped suddenly.

"Did he know Miss Gipson?" she said.

Jerry looked at her. His eyes widened. He said, "For God's sake, Pam!"

"All right," Pam said, "did he?"

Jerry said that they had met, certainly. As he told her. Miss Gipson had gone to see Mr. Hill to talk over

the case he was going to write. He didn't suppose they
had become fast friends from that.

"Or," he said, "fast enemies. Listen, Pam—"

Pam said she was only exploring possibilities.

"Suppose," she said, "Mr. Hill was really talking
about himself. Suppose he really decided that he
wanted to be in danger to . . . what did he say? Face
the bright edge of danger. And suppose he decided that
he might as well begin by killing Miss Gipson."

"Nonsense," Jerry said. "I never heard—"

"And of course," she went on, as if she did not hear
him, "he does profit in a way. He gets a story to write
. . . a very good story. And I think he would appreciate the irony . . . writing up, ostensibly from the
outside, a murder of which he was really the inside.
Speculating about motives, approaching the truth and
shying away from it, tempting discovery and avoiding
it, leaving—"

"Pam!" Jerry said. He spoke very decisively.
"Pam! Alexander Hill is a well-known, reputable professional writer. He has a skilled and trained imagina-
tion, which he uses in his work. He can run up
speculations at the drop of a fact, and does. He is not
a—a thrill murderer."

"Do you *know* he isn't?" Pam said.

"Of course," Jerry told her. She looked at him, and
waited. "Don't be technical," he said. "Of course I
don't *know* he isn't. He just—isn't."

"He was very sure the person who killed Miss
Gipson won't be caught," Pam pointed out. "Why was
he so sure? Unless he had reason to be sure?"

Jerry said that it was a case of the wish being father.
He said Mr. Hill wanted it unsolved, because it
worked out better for him.

"He specializes in unsolved murders," he said and
caught himself, but realized he had not caught himself
in time.

"I wonder if he does," Pam said, gently. Then she
said it was time to feed the cat. She said the cat was
supposed to eat four or five times a day for a while.

"By the way," Jerry said, "how about us?"

They were going out, Pam told him. If they expected to get anything to eat, they were going out. There was barely enough in the house for the little cat.

Inspector O'Malley had been difficult, which was characteristic. He had wanted somebody arrested. It always made him nervous when hours went by without anybody's being arrested. He pointed out that the newspapers were apt to get annoyed; he had said that it was time Weigand used his head.

"We ain't keeping it alive," O'Malley said. "That's the trouble with you, Bill. You don't keep 'em alive. Here it is almost a day after she got knocked off, and where's your morning paper lead?" He had looked at Bill Weigand, but not as if expecting an answer. "They expect it," he said. "I tell them progress, sure. I tell them we are questioning suspects, sure. I tell them she had a niece and a nephew who inherit her money, sure. I tell them we're investigating a couple of letters found in her apartment, sure. But where's the lead?"

Weigand said he was sorry. O'Malley said sure he was sorry. He said that didn't give the mornings a lead, did it? He pointed out that the papers had a lot more space nowadays than they had had and that there couldn't be a better time for a good murder.

"Reflecting credit," he said. "Reflecting credit, lieutenant."

Weigand did not smile. He knew that Inspector O'Malley liked to be the focus of reflected credit. He knew the commissioner liked it, and the mayor. It was to be expected. Elections might depend on it.

"It ain't as if you didn't have evidence, Bill," Inspector O'Malley said, and his tone was confidential and aggrieved. "This teacher who was hanging around—this Spencer. With a fool false name and a grudge against the dame. And no alibi for the girl's killing. At the Library again! Are we supposed to fall for that?"

"He was at the Library," Bill Weigand said. "He

turned in a slip. Bound volumes of *The New Yorker*, October and November, 1932.''

"Why the hell does he want to read that book?" Inspector O'Malley said.

"He says it amuses him," Weigand reported, without inflection.

"Wise cracks," O'Malley said. "Smart Alecks. Hasn't he got anything better to do?"

"Apparently not," Weigand said. "Of course, we don't know what he was doing. He needn't have stayed in the Library. We just know he was there. We're trying to find out more."

"O.K.," O'Malley had said. "How about the girl? This niece. The one who wrote the letter."

So far as they knew, Weigand told him, she was having lunch with her husband at Twenty-one. That was what they said they were doing.

"We're trying to find out more," he said a little wearily. "Also about her brother, who says he ate lunch somewhere on Madison Avenue and doesn't remember the name of the restaurant, but thinks it was between Fiftieth and Fifty-fourth somewhere, and is sure it was on the west side of the street."

"God!" Inspector O'Malley had said, not pleased.

As for Mrs. Willard Burt, who also had written a letter to Miss Gipson, she had been shopping during the time when somebody had shot Florence Adams to death. She had gone to several stores and was not sure when she had been at any of them. There was no corroboration—not even the unsatisfactory one Nora Frost received from her husband; unsatisfactory not because of any lack of emphasis, but because of the source. Willard Burt had been at lunch, alone, a man with whom he had had a business appointment having been unable to make it.

"You go off on the damnedest wild-goose chases sometimes," O'Malley said crossly. "Merely because a couple of women have a misunderstanding and one of them writes a letter to the other, you have to look into it." He looked at Weigand severely. "It's the girl or her brother," he said. "They get the money, don't

they? Or just possibly this schoolteacher, Simpson."
He thawed a little. "Concentrate, Bill," he said. "You
fly all over. Comes from letting the Norths in on
things, probably."

It was, Weigand said, inevitable that they be in on
this, to some extent.

"O.K.," O'Malley said. "But don't pay any attention to them. They're O.K., I guess, but God knows
they're screwy." O'Malley sighed, reflecting. "Always have been," he said. "Leave them out and get on
with it, lieutenant."

Bill had said "yes sir" and gone back to his own
office. Detective Sergeant Stein was waiting for him.
Bill felt momentarily guilty, because Stein had just
been spending several hours investigating a Pam
North hunch—one that even she admitted to be a
hunch.

And his investigation had had no conclusive results.

Mrs. Thomas Merton, daughter of Timothy and
Agatha Fleming, had divorced her husband after a
second jury had failed to make up its mind whether he
was responsible for the fatal epidemic in the big white
house up the Hudson. She had shortly thereafter gone
abroad—that had been late in '29. That was as late into
her life as police records went; she had never returned
to the Fleming house, which had subsequently been
sold through her attorneys. It was not even certain
that she was still alive.

"Obviously," Stein said, "we can check further.
She may have come back any time; she may be living
around the corner. It wouldn't necessarily show up."

That was true, of course. Weigand nodded.

Mrs. Willard Burt had also been abroad between the
wars. She had gone alone as Mrs. Helen Roberts,
widow. She had returned just before the war and had
gone to live in California, where she lived quietly—but
by no means surreptitiously—and alone. She had been
married to Mr. Burt in the spring of 1944 and they had
come to New York. Mr. Burt had lived for some years
in California, comfortably enough in a Los Angeles
apartment. He was generally supposed to be a wid-

ower, although he had never confided details to his acquaintances, who were numerous but apparently not close. He had apparently lived on an entirely adequate income; he invested, conservatively, in the market and was presumed to have enhanced his income somewhat thereby.

There was nothing which made it physically impossible that Helen Merton and Helen Burt were the same person. There was nothing that proved they were. There were pictures of Helen Merton at thirty, and there was nothing in her face or body which made it impossible that she be Helen Burt at forty-seven. Weigand studied the pictured face. The two women— if they were two women—were not different in type. And seventeen years made changes. Were the eyes similarly set? Weigand thought possibly they were. But it was only a possibility. He had a deep distrust of identifications made from photographs; he had seen too many of them made mistakenly. If he had a photograph, taken at approximately the same angle, of Mrs. Burt; if he had the two together; if measurments were made—then he would know more. It might come to that; a sidewalk photographer might snap Mrs. Burt as she left her apartment and they might have the material for comparison. They would see whether it came to that.

He thanked Stein and sent him home to dinner. He sat at his desk, drumming it gently with his fingers and wondered who had killed Amelia Gipson. Then the telephone rang.

"This is John Gipson," the voice said. "I want to see you—now, if possible."

"Why?" Weigand said.

"About Nora," Gipson said. "She's willing for me to tell you about the letter."

"Right," Bill said. "Come along."

"I'm across the street," John Gipson said. "I'll come along."

10

John Gipson looked around Bill Weigand's office, where most things were worn and almost all were a little dusty. He did not seem impressed.

"Look, lieutenant," he said, "I don't want to be rude or anything. But are you the right man to talk to?"

Bill smiled faintly. He said that if it was to talk in answer to a question he had asked, he should think he was.

"What do you want to talk about?" Bill said.

John Gipson said that Weigand knew damn well what he wanted to talk about.

"I want to tell somebody what the letter—why Nora wrote that damn letter," he said. "But I want to tell the right man."

Bill Weigand was patient.

"If you want to talk to the man immediately in charge of the case," he said, "you talk to me. If you want to talk to the man in charge of Homicide, you can talk to Inspector O'Malley. Probably, if you insist, you can talk to the commissioner." He smiled, a little wearily. "And whoever you talk to," he said, "it will come back to me. But suit yourself."

"It's . . . it's nothing to talk about," Gipson said. "Only . . . I suppose we've got to."

If it was about the letter, Weigand said, not hurrying it, it would be very desirable to talk to somebody, and the sooner the better.

"If it hasn't anything to do with your aunt's death," he said, "you will want to cooperate. Obviously. You don't want us to spend time, and energy, digging into something which doesn't mean anything . . . doesn't mean anything to us, for our purposes." He nodded to John Gipson, slowly. "And obviously you're going to say it hasn't anything to do with the murder."

Gipson looked at him thoughtfully.

"I'd like to be in confidence," he said. "Is that possible?"

Weigand shook his head. He said that, obviously, he couldn't promise. If, in spite of what Gipson argued, the police still thought the explanation of the letter had something to do with the case, it wouldn't be confidential. He spoke slowly and carefully, saying what he had often said.

"We don't dig into things for the fun of it," he said. "We don't feed scandal to the newspapers. If you can convince me that whatever you are going to tell me—if you are going to tell me anything—is a private matter and has nothing to do with your aunt's death, whatever you tell me stops with me. But I'll be the one to decide. After I hear it."

Gipson was not satisfied. He did not look satisfied. Weigand waited and the young man sitting beside his desk looked across the room at the wall; he seemed engrossed by a crack in the wall, along which the paint was broken. Weigand did not hurry him. John Gipson started to speak, he still was studying the crack in the wall.

"It was about something that happened up in Maine this summer," he said. "Late in July, I think. I wasn't there. But when Amelia . . . when she threatened to tell Ken . . . Nora told me. The poor kid was . . . hell, she had to tell somebody."

He still looked at the crack in the wall.

"She's a good kid," he said. "A damn good kid. And she's crazy about Ken Frost. Has been for years. They knew each other as kids. He's the only guy she ever remotely fell for. He's . . . he's all she knows. Even now, that's true."

He looked at Weigand then. He said it was a hell of a thing to have to explain. He said he probably wasn't making it clear.

"Hell," he said, "I'm fond of the kid. That's why she . . . told me. That's why I'm here."

"Right," Weigand said. "You're doing all right, Mr. Gipson."

Gipson shook his head. He said he didn't think so. He said that, however, he put it, Weigand was going to get a wrong idea of the kid.

"There used to be words for it," he said. "Words with . . . oh, definite meanings. I could just say she was a good kid. You know?"

Weigand said, again, that he got the picture. Still he did not hurry John Gipson.

"A good kid and in love with Ken," John Gipson repeated. "It's . . . it's embarrassing to talk about your sister."

He was rather likable, Weigand thought. But he did not say so. He did not even commit his own mind to the view.

John Gipson looked again at the crack in the paint on the wall. He continued to look at it as he spoke.

"Late in July, up in Maine, Nora met a man," he said. "I don't know much about him . . . just an ordinary sort of guy, I guess. I think he was in the Army and on leave . . . one of those thirty-day jobs, I guess. He was a couple of years older than Nora and . . . oh, just an ordinary sort of nice guy. You know what I mean?"

"Yes," Bill said. "I get the picture, Mr. Gipson."

"He didn't mean a damn thing to Nora and I don't suppose she meant much more to him," John Gipson said, and his eyes still regarded the wall. He spoke slowly, picking his words.

"Since Ken had been gone she'd gone around, of course," he said. "I mean, she'd gone to lunch and things like that with men they both knew, or friends . . . or . . . well, just the usual run of guys you meet. Mostly in parties, of course. But if she met somebody on the street she knew and he invited her to lunch and she wasn't tied up, she'd go to lunch. Like anybody."

"Right," Bill Weigand said. His voice indicated that it was all right.

"So when she met this guy in Maine, because he knew some people we knew and was an O. K. guy, she saw him now and then. As she would have if Ken had been here, as far as that goes. There wasn't anything more than that, to begin with." He paused again, and then turned suddenly to Bill Weigand. "There wasn't anything more than that at any time," he said, and he spoke emphatically. "That's what I won't be able to get across. It was just. . . ." He broke off and looked unhappy. After a moment of waiting, Bill made a suggestion.

"Suppose you try to forget this is your sister you're talking about, Mr. Gipson," he said. "I think you're running into . . . a taboo or something. Pretend this is just any nice girl you know, in love with her husband overseas, meeting a presentable young man in the summer on vacation, going swimming with him probably, having a drink or two with him. None of it having anything to do with her and her husband."

John Gipson listened and toward the end he nodded. He said he supposed Weigand was ahead of him; he said he supposed it was all obvious as hell.

"Only," he said, "it doesn't seem obvious to Nora, and so it doesn't to me. She isn't just some . . . some nice girl you've met a couple of times and can call by name. She's somebody I'm fond of. She's somebody . . . different."

That, Bill told him, was natural. Things were obvious only when they happened to other people. They were not not obvious to you, when you were in them, or when people close to you were in them. Old stories are old stories only in the abstract, Bill said.

"Yes," Gipson said. "That's the way it is. It's hard to explain. It would be easier if you knew Nora. She's not. . . ." He broke off again and suddenly seemed angry. "You'll think she's a push-over, damn it all," he said. "and she's never been in love with anybody but Ken. Not in love . . . in any way. It was just something that happened, God knows how."

It wasn't hard to understand, Bill told him, when the difficulty of making himself clear stopped John Gipson again.

"You have two healthy kids on vacation," Bill said. "Good-looking kids. They're by themselves, in the sun, maybe, or some warm night on the beach. And all at once they look damned good to one another. One of them's a girl with her husband gone a long time . . . and . . . well, among other things, curiosity. Say she's never played around at all; not even as much as most. Say she's fallen in love with one man when she was a kid, and married him, and stayed in love with him. Still she'd wonder. And set things up just right, some time and some place . . . maybe after a couple of drinks . . . and I mean a couple . . . and . . . there you are. Sister or no sister, Gipson." He smiled suddenly. "Hell," he said, and for a moment he was not apparently a policeman. "It's not a tragedy. Even to Frost it wouldn't be, if he's worth a damn. It's . . . just one of the things that happen."

Gipson nodded.

"Of course," he said, "you're assuming it did happen."

"Naturally," Bill Weigand told him. "More or less as I say. Didn't it?"

"Yes," Gipson said. "Pretty much as you say. And Amelia found out."

"How?" Bill asked him.

Gipson shrugged faintly.

"She didn't say," he told Bill. "But they didn't tell her, certainly. They were both . . . they both wished it hadn't happened. Nora particularly . . . she wished like hell it hadn't happened. But she didn't go into a tail spin, actually. Or if she did, she came out of it. She's not a schoolgirl. Making allowances for everything—her emotions, all that—she could figure it out more or less the way we do. She didn't go around mooning about it. And certainly she wouldn't confide in Amelia . . . didn't confide in Amelia. And—I don't know what you'll think of this, but it seems O.K. to me—she wasn't going to blurt it out to Ken. To make it all right with herself; fix her conscience up."

"Right," Bill said. "There are several schools of thought. But I'd play it that way, if I were your sister."

You couldn't tell unless it were your own problem, Gipson said. But he thought he'd play it that way. And, anyhow, it was up to her. But Amelia found out.

"I can only think of one way," he said. "Since nobody told her that we know of. Somebody . . . hell, somebody saw them. Maybe Amelia herself. She snooped a good deal. They were on a beach, and . . . well, somehow they got separated from the others. I . . . I suppose they couldn't help themselves. I suppose that, without knowing it, they wanted to get separated from the others."

Gipson was trying to work it out for himself; trying to explain it to himself, Bill thought. He would go on trying for quite a while, probably. So would his sister, a good deal more acutely.

"Anyway," Bill said, "your aunt did find out. And then?"

"She told Nora she'd found out," Gipson said. "It . . . it must have been quite a scene. Amelia had strong views about morality, you know. Like some old maids have. Hers were unusually strong views, I always thought, and she was never one to make allowances. So it must have been quite a scene. Nora didn't go into it much. Except that Amelia insisted Nora tell Ken about it, at once."

"Because it was the only right thing to do," Bill said. "Of course."

Gipson said that was it. Because it was the right thing to do. No matter how many people got hurt; no matter how little good it did anybody.

"Nora's pretty honest," Gipson said. "She could have pretended to agree . . . as far as that goes, she could have pretended she *had* told Ken. That would have put it off. But instead she said she wasn't going to tell Ken. So Amelia said that in that case she would. And Nora said, in effect, over her dead body."

He broke off and his eyes widened somewhat.

"Over Nora's dead body, I mean," he said. "Even so, it doesn't sound so good, does it?"

Bill Weigand didn't go into how it sounded.

"And?" he said.

"Well," Gipson said, "about that time Ken got shifted and Nora managed, somehow, not to let Amelia know his new address. I suppose if she had, Amelia would have cabled him. 'Nora unfaithful. Think you should know,' probably. But there was no hiding that he was coming home pretty soon, and Amelia said she would tell him then. First time she saw him, probably. Makes a pretty picture, doesn't it? You can see why Nora isn't . . . wasn't . . . too fond of her aunt."

He broke off, and looked at Weigand, waiting comment.

"And hence the letter," Weigand said.

"Hence the letter," Gipson agreed. "You'll see it fits. You'll see—anyhow I hope you will—how the kid came to write as she did."

Weigand nodded.

"Right," he said. He paused. He went on, "And of course you see where it leaves her," he said. "Her aunt was going to tell Major Frost something he might not be able to take; something that might destroy your sister's marriage. Or that she might be afraid would. You see how it looks—in the abstract, that is. Amelia Gipson was killed before she got a chance to see Major Frost."

There was a very long pause, then. John Gipson returned to his intent gaze at the wall. When he spoke, it was dully.

"Oh," he said, "I get it. So does Nora, for that matter. But she was the one who wanted you told . . . some time when Ken wasn't around. She couldn't tell you this afternoon, obviously. I—to be honest—I thought maybe we could get away with not telling you. But I suppose she was right."

"Oh yes," Weigand said. "She was right. As far as that goes."

Well, Gipson said, there they had it. It was on the table, face up. All at once, Weigand thought, he seemed rather relieved. He was almost cheerful when he spoke again.

"So now we're both in it," he said. "Nora and me. She to keep the awful truth from Ken. I to get money for my new invention. Motives. No alibis I know of."

"Right," Weigand agreed, equably. "Motives. No alibis for the killing of the chambermaid. And since we have no real idea when poison was substituted for medicine in your aunt's apartment, nobody has any alibi for that."

"Well," Gipson said, "What do you do now?"

"I just keep on poking into things, Mr. Gipson," Bill told him. "That's all. Picking up what I can, where I can. Trying to make it all fit in."

There seemed to be no answer to that that John Gipson could think of.

"Well," he said, "do you want me any longer?" He stood up.

"No," Bill told him. "Not unless you've something more to tell me."

Gipson began to shake his head. Then he stopped and said there might be one thing.

"You want to pick up what you can," he said. "How about a chap named Spencer, Philip Spencer?"

"Well," Weigand said, "what about Spencer?"

"I don't know," Gipson said. "He says he was there. He knew Amelia."

Mr. Spencer had been there, Weigand agreed. He had known Amelia Gipson.

"Only," he said, "how do you know? Because we haven't given it out. When did he say that?"

"When he called Nora up," Gipson said. "Right after you left this afternoon. To—what did he say? Offer his condolences." Gipson paused, reflecting. "Nora said he didn't sound as if meant it."

"You mean," Bill said, "that Mr. Spencer called up

a perfectly strange person to express his sympathy at her loss of an aunt?" He made it sound unlikely; he thought it sounded unlikely.

Gipson shook his head.

"Not a perfectly strange person, actually," he said. "He used to teach English or something at Ward College, out in Indiana—where Amelia taught, you know. And Nora went there for a couple of years. She had some classes under Mr. Spencer and, of course, Amelia's being on the faculty got Nora to knowing a good many of the teachers better than she would otherwise."

Bill Weigand was interested. His interest was not reflected in his voice when he said he had not known that Nora went to Ward College.

"Oh yes," John Gipson said. "Amelia persuaded father. I don't know . . . maybe Amelia got a commission, or something. Maybe she just wanted Nora under her eyes. Nora got out after a couple of years."

Weigand said, without echoing the assertion in his tone, that it was interesting. He asked when Nora had been at Ward's.

"Let's see," Gipson said. "The year before the war started. And the next year. That would be '40-'41 and '41-'42."

"Right," Weigand said.

"You know Amelia got Spencer kicked out of his job?" Gipson said.

"Oh yes," Bill Weigand said. "I know that, Mr. Gipson."

He regarded Gipson, and now he was abstracted.

"Did Spencer ask to come around and convey his condolences in person?" he wanted to know.

Not exactly, Gipson told him. But he had said he would like to attend the funeral services the next afternoon. Tomorrow.

Bill Weigand received this information without comment. He nodded abstractedly when Gipson said that if there wasn't anything else, he was going to get himself some dinner. Abstractedly, he watched Gipson go. Sergeant Mullins came in, as if he had been waiting to come in. He looked tired and rather morose.

"Listen, loot," he said. "All those people who was at the Library. Did you expect to get anything out of them?"

"Not particularly," Bill Weigand told him.

"O.K.," Mullins said. "Because so far as I can see, you ain't goin' to. You want the details?"

On a hundred and thirty-three people? Weigand wanted to know. He shuddered slightly.

"After all, sergeant," he said, "you're a sergeant. I'm a lieutenant. What's the theory of the executive? Leave details to subordinates. You, Mullins, are a subordinate."

Mullins said that Weigand was telling him. He said it somewhat morosely.

"Therefore," Bill told him, "I leave the people at the Library to you—all of them. And what do you get."

"Nothin'," Mullins said, still morose. "The boys have seen most of them and I've seen the boys' reports. Nothin'."

"Right," Bill said. "Then we wash them up?"

"Yeah," Mullins said. "Unless you want—"

Weigand said he didn't.

"O.K., loot," Mullins said. "The guy who was just in here . . . was that the nephew? Gipson?"

It had been, Bill told him. Briefly, he sketched John Gipson's story. When he had finished, Mullins whistled. He thought and whistled again.

"You know, loot," he said, "every time the Norths get into—"

Bill grinned. He said he knew. He said he had heard it before.

"Now we got, how many?" Mullins said. "Spencer, because he was sore at the Gipson dame for getting him thrown out of his job. O.K.?"

Bill agreed. His finger ticked off one on the desk top. "And he may attribute the death of his wife to the loss of his job," he added. Mullins said, "Yeah."

"Two," Mullins said, "Gipson. Because he wanted the money. Which is good enough for me."

"Right," Weigand said. "It's good. And we could figure that all this carefully told story about his sister is told primarily to put us on her trail, and take us off his. He may have insisted that it be told, although he says she did."

Mullins said that that would be a lousy trick to play on a sister. Bill pointed out that sodium fluoride was a lousy trick to play on any auntie. Mullins said, "Yeah."

"Three is the sister," Weigand said, then. "Assuming it all happened just as Gipson says it did. Assuming she is as much in love with her husband as he thinks she is. Assuming she's very emotional, has been very stirred up during the last few years, as who hasn't, that she saw only one way of keeping her aunt from talking. It might add up to murder."

"Hell yes," Mullins said. "If she's that kinda dame."

They didn't know, Bill said, what kinda dame she was.

"She's pretty and young and emotional," he said. "I never found any way to pick out people who would kill. Did you? She's just a pretty girl, so far as I can see, who always had enough money, went to pretty good schools, knew the right people." He paused, considering. "I suppose Ward is a pretty good school," he said. He spoke abstractedly. "She went there, according to her brother."

Mullins pointed out that that was reasonable enough. After all, her aunt taught there. Weigand did not answer, but sat looking across his desk at nothing. Mullins looked at him and saw an expression he had seen before. He waited, and after a time he said, "You got something, loot?"

Weigand came back slowly. He shook his head, but he seemed doubtful. He said they were running into coincidences.

"Sure," Mullins said. "Life's full of them." He sighed. "Damn nuisance, too. Fixes it so you don't know where you're going half the time."

Bill nodded, but he still seemed to be thinking of

something else. When he spoke it was slowly, thought-fully.

"Remember Spencer got kicked out because he was caught fooling around with some girl?" he said. "Or, according to his version, some girl misunderstood what was merely professional friendliness and went to Miss Gipson. Remember?"

"Sure," Mullins said. " 'Some spiteful little fool,' he said the girl was."

"Right," Weigand said. "What I was thinking was—it would be interesting if Nora Frost, who was Nora Gipson then, was the spiteful little fool. And if Spencer called up today just to let her know he was around. Because, if he's a little touched on the subject—and he could be—he might have a grudge against the girl who got him in the jam. If Nora's the girl. What do you think of that, sergeant?"

Mullins thought of it. He asked if Weigand had anything to hang it on? Bill shook his head.

"It would be a hell of a note," Mullins decided. "Because now maybe he'd be gunning for her—for the girl. Maybe he'd figure one down, one to go."

"Right," Bill said. "Maybe he would."

The telephone bell rang then and Bill listened, speaking infrequently. Once he looked at his watch. At the end, he said, "Right. About fifteen minutes." He replaced the receiver.

"We're having dinner with the Norths, sergeant," he said. "At Charles."

"Swell," Mullins said, looking as if he thought it was swell.

"Yes," Bill Weigand said, gently. "Yes. You see, Mrs. North thinks she has a new suspect for us."

"Oh," Sergeant Mullins said. After he had said it, he left his mouth slightly open.

As he stood up to go, Bill Weigand looked down at his desk. The photograph of Mrs. Helen Merton, taken when she was thirty, stared up at him. Even if Pam North had a new suspect now, she might be interested in it, he thought. He put the photograph in an envelope and the envelope in his pocket.

11

Wednesday, 8:20 P.M.
to Thursday, 11 A.M.

Pam and Jerry North had taken their drinks to a table in a corner of the café section at Charles. Hugo took Weigand and Sergeant Mullins to the table, although Mullins looked backward, a little wistfully, at the bar.

"Hello, Bill," Pam said. "We've got a new cat. It looks like a very tiny polar bear, doesn't it, Jerry?"

"Exactly," Jerry said. "Did you tell Hugo what you wanted?"

"Hugo knows," Pam said. "I told him what they were going to want. Martini. Old-fashioned. The cat's Martini."

"What?" said Mullins.

"That's the cat's name," Pam said. She looked thoughtful. "But I'm afraid she's going to have a confused life," she said. "Because when anybody wants one she'll think it's her and around our house that would be confusing, I should think. Especially as she already looks like a polar bear."

"What?" Weigand said.

"Well," Pam told him, "that would be confusing enough, wouldn't it? To look like a bear and be called after a drink, and all the time to be a cat?"

"Oh," Bill said. He paused. "I thought it was a new suspect, not a new cat," he said. "Not that I'm not glad you've got another cat, Pam."

"Well," Pam said, "Jerry's almost talked me out of

144

it. The suspect, I mean. But what would you think of Alexander Hill?"

Bill Weigand looked blank. He said he wouldn't think anything, having no idea who Alexander Hill was.

"A smallish man with a very black beard," Pam said. "He writes. About murders."

"Oh," Bill said. It might have meant anything.

"It's a lot of nonsense, Bill," Jerry North said. "Pam knows it is."

"All the same," Pam said, "he talked very oddly."

"He's a very odd man," Jerry told her. "He didn't talk oddly, for him."

Bill Weigand suggested they let him in on it. They let him in on it.

"You mean to say," Bill said, "that you think he killed Amelia Gipson because her murder would make a good story for the book?" He looked at Pam with doubt. "Really?" he said.

Pam said it sounded foolish that way. She thought it over. She said it sounded flippant. She said Bill was leaving out two points. Hill's certainty that the crime would not be solved. His obvious interest—relish, almost—when he talked of murder as such, and the excitement of committing it. She said there was also something more. Something indefinable. An attitude. She said Bill would have to give her that.

Bill nodded. He said that, since he had not been there, he would give her the attitude.

"But," he said, "you have to know a person very well to—sort out their attitudes. What you took for an attitude may be a mannerism. Do you know him very well?"

"No," Pam said. "Jerry knows him better."

"Well," Bill said, "did he have an attitude, Jerry?"

Jerry paused a moment and then said he knew what Pam meant. But he said, also, that he didn't know Hill well enough to know whether it was a mannerism. He said that, obviously, he had not been convinced by Pam's theory, since he had tried to argue her out of it.

"As for the interest in murder, per se," Bill said,

"he makes his living by it, I gather. By writing about it. So he has theories. The one he spun for you isn't unusual; it's quite popular in literary circles. De Quincey. That sort of thing." He paused, reflecting. "Except for Leopold and Loeb," he said, "I don't remember running into it outside books. And they were—"

He paused, seeking words.

"Otherwise peculiar," Pam North said. "I know. And Mr. Hill certainly isn't that."

Bill nodded. And as for the writer's assurance that the case would not be solved, there was a school of writers which held that the police never solved anything. Which, he added mildly, was untrue. They solved most things. Private detectives got divorce evidence. They got back stolen jewelry by making dickers the police couldn't make. They investigated applicants for surety bonds. It was, he said, a matter of machinery.

"For example," he said, "fifty or more men, all of them trained, some of them fairly bright, have been working on this case. Part of the time; all of the time. They've been interviewing practically everyone who was in the Library when she collapsed there. They've gone over the apartment house she lived in. They've taken hundreds of fingerprints and run them through the files, looking for somebody we know. They've been checking into the lives of everyone concerned. Out in California, they've been checking up on the Burts, because Mrs. Burt wrote a letter to Miss Gipson. They've checked up on the handwriting in the letter, just to make sure she did write it. They've checked—are still checking—on Major Frost, to see if he was really in Kansas City instead of New York yesterday afternoon. The precinct men have just about taken apart the hotel in which Florence Adams was killed—and incidentally, we've picked up a couple of men we've been anxious to meet for quite some time. They've interviewed people who work and live within earshot of the hotel, trying to find somebody who did hear a shot and knows what time he heard it, because if we come to a trial we'll want to pin that down if we can. At the laboratory over in Brooklyn they've put the slug that killed the girl through all the tests there are, and if we find the .25 caliber German automatic it came from we'll greet it like a brother. Precinct men have been trying to find out where John Gipson had lunch today and if anybody can swear he did, and whether the Frosts had lunch at Twenty-one and when. Out in Indiana, men are checking up on Philip Spencer and trying to find out why, exactly, he lost his job—and who the student was he was supposed to have made passes at. Up in Maine—"

"Look," Jerry said mildly, "who are you arguing with, Bill? Your drink's getting warm."

Bill Weigand broke off, looked at Jerry a moment without apparently seeing him, looked at his drink and finished it. They looked at the menus, then, and ordered.

"I don't know what got me started on that," Bill said, when Fritz had gone off to get them food. "Only people somehow get the idea that chasing criminals is a one-man job—just because newspapermen and everybody else find it easier to write about it that way. It's—it's a mass movement."

"Why Maine?" Pam said.

They all looked at her.

"What are they looking for in Maine?" she said. "You said 'up in Maine' and then Jerry interrupted you."

Oh yes, Bill said, that. He said that John Gipson had explained his sister's letter and that his explanation could stand checking in Maine. He stopped.

"Well?" Pam said.

"Period," Bill said. "Confidential, unless it means something. By agreement with young Gipson."

Pam said, "Oh." She said "all right."

"Of course," she said, "I suppose Amelia had found out something about her niece and was going to tell her niece's husband. Something about a man. Apparently a man in Maine."

"What makes you think that?" Bill said. His voice was, he thought, noncommittal.

Pam said that was the way the letter sounded.

"And," she said, "you're transparent, Bill. Actually, I just threw it out. You should have heard yourself keep expression out of your voice."

Bill Weigand said, "Oh."

Fritz came back with the food. They ate, making small remarks between bites, chiefly to prove that they were too civilized to obey the human instinct to put first things first. Pam finished and lighted a cigarette.

"About Mr. Hill," she said, "I really still like Mrs. Burt better. What have you found out about her, or is that confidential, too?"

Bill Weigand reached across and took a cigarette out of Pam's pack. He said it wasn't confidential. He told them what they had found out about Mrs. Burt, her recent history, her marriage. And he pulled the photograph out of his pocket and gave it to Pam. She looked at it, and then she looked at Bill and raised her eyebrows. Jerry North took the photograph from her and looked at it, and then he, too, looked at Bill.

"Well," Pam said, "who is it?"

"Is it anybody you ever saw?" Bill asked her. She took the photograph back from Jerry and looked at it again.

"I don't know," she said. "Is it?"

"If your theory about Helen Burt is true, it's a picture of her seventeen years ago, when she was Helen Merton," he said, "Is it?"

Pam looked at the photograph carefully. She said clothes were funny, even seventeen years ago. She put the photograph down in front of her and looked off into space. Then she looked back at Bill.

"I don't know," she said. "What do you think?"

"I don't know either," Bill said. "There's no apparent reason—like a long nose, or a harelip or anything—why it couldn't be. I'd even say there was a general similarity."

Pam nodded. She said she would, too.

"The age is the trouble, partly," she said. "People

change so, unless you know them very well. In pictures, particularly."

"Huh?" Mullins said, emerging suddenly from food.

"Hello, sergeant," Pam said. "Enjoy yourself?"

"Yeah," Mullins said. "What do you mean people change if you don't know them, Mrs. North?"

"Only," she said, "if you know very well what people look like now, you can pick them out then. But you have to."

"Oh," Mullins said. He thought it over. "Sure," he said. He looked at Bill Weigand.

"Obviously," Bill told him, gravely. "Very clearly put."

"Oh," Mullins said. He looked at his plate, which looked back at him blankly.

"Have you got a picture of her now?" Pam asked.

Bill Weigand shook his head. He said they didn't have yet. He said they could get one; he said they probably would.

"You think it's a digression, don't you?" Pam said. Bill nodded.

"Who *do* you think?" she said.

Bill Weigand lifted his shoulders.

"No hunch," he said. "For your use only, Pam. Not to be quoted. The odds are on one of the kids. I'd say on Gipson. He wanted money. If his aunt died he'd have money. That's where the odds always are."

"Or his sister," Jerry said. "If she had a good enough motive—this mysterious motive."

"That isn't mysterious," Pam said. "It's merely confidential. Is she in love with her husband, Bill?"

"Am I Dorothy Dix?" Bill said. Pam merely waited. "For a guess—yes," he said. "For a guess, he's in love with her."

"And the man in Maine?" Pam said.

"What man in Maine?" Bill wanted to know.

"By all means," Pam said. "Be confidential. I take it you won't buy Mr. Hill?"

"No," Bill Weigand said.

"Or this former professor—Spencer?" That was from Jerry.

Bill said he had told them he didn't have a hunch. He said Spencer was obviously in the running. He had merely given them the odds.

"Not counting Mr. Hill," Pam said, "we have how many? The nephew and niece. That's two. Mr. Spencer, that's three. Will you count Mrs. Burt?"

Certainly he would count Mrs. Burt; Bill Weigand told her.

"Because she could be Helen Merton, or just because she wrote the letter?" Pam said.

Because she wrote the letter, Weigand told her. When you boiled it down, there was no reason whatever to think she was Helen Merton.

"Or any of the things you think," he added. "That it was really she who killed her family, and that Amelia Gipson knew her before and identified her, *and* found something which had been missed earlier to throw suspicion on her. It's pure—hypothesis."

But, Pam reminded him, he had gone to the trouble to get the photograph. Bill said it was very little trouble; he said he wouldn't deny his curiosity had been aroused.

"Can I keep the picture?" Pam said. "Maybe something'll come to me."

Bill nodded. He said he was sure something would come to her.

"It always does," Jerry said. "Something."

"You two," Pam said. "Are you coming to look at the cat, Bill?"

"I'm going home to look at a bed," he said.

"How's Dorian?" Pam asked him.

Bill said Dorian was fine—and out of town.

"I'm going home to sleep," he said. Pam said, "Oh."

The Norths walked home slowly, not talking much. Pam said she thought Bill was stuck, and Jerry said that he would probably come unstuck, since he usually did. In the apartment, the kitten talked to them sternly, but forgot to be aggrieved when they sat down and it could climb to Jerry's shoulder and, from there, bite his ear.

"She likes your flavor," Pam said, watching them. "That's good."

Jerry took the little cat from his shoulder and put it on Pam's, which was conveniently within reach. The little cat bit Pam's ear.

"And yours," Jerry said, contentedly, as Pam said, "Ouch!" "For that matter—"

"I think," Pam said, "that it's bedtime for small cats. Come on, Martini. I've given her the guest-room," she said. "I think she ought to have a room of her own."

She put the little cat in the guest room and came back and sat down beside Jerry. When she leaned back, her head rested on his shoulder. She leaned back.

Jerry North looked at the headlines in *The Times* and then at the book page. Orville Prescott had reviewed the wrong book. But the advertisement had a good spot. Jerry put the paper down, poured himself another cup of coffee and looked at Pam. She was studying the photograph. He continued to look at her, with approval, and she looked up.

"Well," he said, "have you made up your mind?"

Pam shook her head.

"I'll have to go look at her," she said. "Or wait until Bill gets a photograph of her now."

Jerry advised the latter. He said it might be a little complicated to go to Mrs. Burt and say you wanted to look at her because she might be a murderer.

"Oh," Pam said, "I'd have to have an excuse, of course. I left my vanity. I mean my compact."

"Did you?" Jerry said. "The silver one?"

"No," Pam said. "The one I got because I left the silver one somewhere else. Only then I found it again. I'm very careful with it now. This was the other one."

"Did you leave it at the Burts'?" Jerry said.

"Somewhere," Pam said. "It might have been the Burts'. Actually it was probably your office, and you might have somebody look. But I don't know it wasn't the Burts'."

"I wouldn't," Jerry said.

Pam said she knew he wouldn't. The question was, should she?

"No," Jerry said. "You shouldn't."

Pam said she didn't see what harm would come of it. Jerry said she never saw what harm would come of it. But harm sometimes did.

"Never really," Pam reassured him. "Only almost."

"Once I got a broken arm," Jerry said. "And once I got banged on the head. And once you got chased by—"

"I know," Pam said. "That's what I mean. Only almost. He didn't catch me."

He had, Jerry told her, come too damn near.

"This is a frail woman in her late forties," Pam said. "What could she do to me? Even if she wanted to? And if I look at her and she isn't, then we're out of it, because it's the only hunch I have."

"Mr. Hill?" Jerry said.

Pamela North shook her head. She said she had about given up Mr. Hill.

"Well," Jerry said, "I wish you'd leave Mrs. Burt to Bill."

Bill was not interested, Pam told him. That was the trouble. She might as well cross Mrs. Burt out, if she was out.

Jerry looked at his watch, made sounds of consternation and stood up. He kissed the back of Pam's neck, told her to be good, and started for the door.

"Wait a minute," Pam said. "The cat's on you."

Jerry stopped and took Martini off his right shoulder. Martini clung and scolded. He put her on Pam's right shoulder and she began to purr. It was only when he was in a cab on the way to his office that Jerry remembered he had planned to get Pam to promise not to go look at Mrs. Burt.

"Mrs. Burt is not in," the maid told Pamela North. "I don't expect her—"

"Oh," Pam said. "I'm sorry. I—"

"I'm sorry," the maid said. "Shall I say you called, Miss—er—Mrs.—"

"North," Pam said. Then she rather wished she hadn't, because Mrs. Burt, when the maid told her, would wonder why Mrs. North had called.

"I think I left my compact when I was here yesterday," Pam said. "With Leiutenant Weigand, you know. And I happened to be passing and just thought I'd—"

"I don't think so," the maid said. "I'd have seen it when I straightened up. What kind of a compact was it?"

"Plastic," Pam said. "With a monogram. PN."

"No," the maid said. "I don't think so, Mrs. Nord."

"North," Pam said. "In that case, don't bother Mrs. Burt."

"Good morning, Mrs. North," a slow and calm voice said. Mr. Burt was standing in the door from the living room to the foyer. "Won't you come in? I heard something about a compact."

Pam told him about the compact. She said the compact apparently wasn't there.

"Well," Willard Burt said, "we must be sure of that, Mrs. North. Perhaps we can find it. It may have slipped down somewhere." He spoke very deliberately, so that there seemed to be tiny pauses between the words. It reminded Mrs. North of the way someone else spoke, but she did not remember who it was. She thought chiefly that she was now faced with a probably exhaustive search for a compact which was almost certainly somewhere else. And that she was wasting time, since she would not get to look at Mrs. Burt. She said it wasn't important enough to bother about, and Mr. Burt said that of course it was important enough to bother about.

"In any event it is no bother," he said. He waited then, expectantly, and Pam went in.

"I was sitting here," she said, going to the chair. "It may just have slipped down behind the cushion, of course." She moved the cushion and looked. "It didn't," she said. "I must have left it somewhere else. I'm always leaving them around, Jerry says."

Mr. Burt looked several places. He said that it appeared she must have left it somewhere else.

"As your husband said," he told her. "I assume, in any event, that the Jerry you speak of is Mr. North?"

"Yes," Pam said.

"His must be an interesting occupation," Mr. Burt said. "Tracking down the perpetrators of crime."

"What?" Pam said. "Oh—no. Jerry's a publisher. North Books, Inc. He's not a detective."

Mr. Burt said he had jumped to conclusions. A foolish habit of his. Because she was a detective, he had assumed that her husband also was.

"But I'm not either," Pam assured him. "We just know a detective. Bill Weigand. Sometimes we just— oh, we get involved, somehow. Because we know him, usually. But this time, of course, because Miss Gipson worked for Jerry. Doing research, you know."

"Of course," Willard Burt said. "I read that in the newspapers. North Books, too. I didn't make the connection."

There was no reason why he should, Pam told him. She thanked him for his help, and apologized for the bother. She moved toward the door. But Mr. Burt did not follow her.

"It seems to be a very interesting case," he said. "Not that I know much about murder cases. But naturally, since Helen had written that letter which the police misconstrued, I've been reading about this one. I trust Lieutenant Weigand is making progress?"

Again the methodical manner of his speech reminded Pam of someone else, and again she could not remember of whom it reminded her.

"Oh yes," she said. "Of course, much of it is confidential. Our being friends with Bill doesn't change that. Like a doctor."

"What?" Mr. Burt said.

"Like being friends with a doctor," Pam told him. "Naturally, a doctor doesn't tell much about his cases, and no names. It's that way with a detective, too."

Mr. Burt agreed that that was natural.

"One thing that struck me," he said, "was the coincidence. That she was, in a sense, investigating murder when she was murdered. An ironic touch."

Mr. Burt wanted to talk, apparently. It was to be expected. It would be natural for him to wonder about a case in which his wife was involved; about which his wife had been questioned. It was natural that he should try to pump her. And it occurred to Pam that, since she couldn't do what she had come to do, she might pick up something from Mr. Burt. Because, if his wife had been Helen Merton, he might very well know it; he would almost certainly know it.

Pam agreed that it was ironic. Her tone did not close the conversation.

"Of course," Willard Burt said, "the police have no doubt thought of that. But I wondered whether she might not possibly have happened on something in one of the old cases that was—well, perhaps dangerous to know. But no doubt the police have thought of that possibility."

"Oh yes," Pam said. "I think they have. But I don't think they are really very convinced it was that way."

Probably, Willard Burt said, there was a much simpler explanation; a more direct explanation. He supposed that, in such cases, the police looked first to see who would profit. The niece and nephew in this case.

"Although," he said, "my wife's met them and thinks them quite charming young people. However, I suppose even charming people—"

He let that hang. Pamela nodded.

"Of course," she said, when he did not continue, "I don't really know any more about it than you do, Mr. Burt. But I thought the—coincidence—you spoke of was very interesting. I'm glad somebody agrees. Because it does seem possible she stumbled on something—oh, say in the Fleming case. Or the Wentworth case."

"Fleming?" Mr. Burt said. "I don't think I ever heard of the Fleming case."

"A doctor named Merton," Pam told him. She

looked at him with interest, and tried not to let interest show in her eyes. "He was accused of killing his wife's family. With typhoid germs. They never proved he had."

She could not see any change in Mr. Burt's face as she spoke.

"No," he said, "I never heard of that one. Or—what was it—Wentworth?"

Pam told him, briefly, of the Wentworth case. Midway, he nodded.

"Yes," he said, "I did hear of that one, although I was in California at the time. She was a very beautiful girl, from her pictures."

Pam agreed she had been.

"Actually," Mr. Burt said, "wasn't Miss Gipson reading about a poison case when she was taken ill? It seemed to me there was something like that in one account I read."

Pam nodded.

"That was really coincidence," she said. "She was reading about another woman who had been poisoned with sodium fluoride. A Mrs. Purdy. By her husband, they thought."

Mr. Burt looked as if he were trying to pin down an elusive memory.

"Purdy," he said. "Purdy. It seems to me—wasn't he later killed? When he was trying to escape the police?"

That was it, Pam said. Mr. Burt, although he did not, seemed to snap his fingers.

"I remember now," he said. "He slipped up, somehow. I remember reading about it. Couldn't explain why he had the poison around, or something like that."

"No roaches," Pam said. "It was sodium fluoride, too, and you use it for roaches."

"That's right," Mr. Burt said. "I don't know how I came to remember that. I suppose because it was—such a trivial thing. Such a silly way for him to fail." He nodded, apparently pleased with his memory.

"Perhaps whoever killed Miss Gipson will make some such silly slip. I'm sure we all hope so."

Pam agreed they did. There seemed to be no way, now, to prolong the discussion, or to get it back to the Merton case. She stood up, and decided to have another try.

"It's odd you don't remember the Merton case," she said. "It was very widely written up. Mrs. Merton apparently thought her husband was guilty, because after the second trial, she got a divorce. I suppose she stood by as long as she could."

"Women do that," Mr. Burt said. "So often."

It was a pious sentiment—and a sentimental tribute. But it was not what Pam wanted.

"I've sometimes wondered," she said, "how it must have influenced her life. Such a dreadful situation—the man you were married to, accused of murdering your parents and brothers and sisters. Dreadful, particularly if you thought he had—or knew he had."

"Very dreadful," Mr. Burt agreed. "A very—unhappy situation for any woman. But it was a long time ago." He paused. "At least," he said, "I assume it was a long time ago. From the way you speak of it."

"Seventeen years," Pam told him. "Mrs. Merton was thirty."

Mr. Burt nodded.

"Of course," he said, "thirty seems quite young to me, Mrs. North. Much younger than it must to you. And seventeen years is a long time. Probably she has rebuilt her life, somehow."

Pam said she supposed so.

"Probably I'm wasting my sympathy," she said. "Probably she's married again and happy and it's all like—oh, like some story she read a long time ago. I suppose things fade out, finally."

Mr. Burt nodded, in agreement.

"They do," he said. "I assure you they do, Mrs. North. Unless something happens to bring them up again—and it always seems a pity to me when something does. Probably your Mrs. Merton has a new life now and has almost forgotten the old tragedy." He shook his head. "It is too bad that this brings it up again, even so slightly," he said. "We can only hope she doesn't read the papers—if she is still alive."

They were both standing, now, and it was clearly time for Pam to go. She went, while Mr. Burt slowly murmured hopes that she would find the compact she had lost; regrets that their search had been a waste of time.

It had been a waste of time, all right, Pam thought as she waved at a taxicab and saw it pull toward her. She had not seen Mrs. Burt, so she knew no more than before whether the picture in her bag was a likeness of Mrs. Burt at thirty, as well as of Helen Merton at thirty. And, although maybe she had missed something, she couldn't see that she had got anything out of Mr. Burt. Either he was a good actor or she was barking up a wrong tree.

"Woof!" Mrs. North said, experimentally.

The taxicab driver half turned in his seat.

"Beg pardon?" he said. His expression was surprised and, Pam thought, a little alarmed.

"I just cleared my throat," Pam said. She cleared it officially. "I must have swallowed something," she told him.

12

The grist continued to come in. Looking at it, Bill Weigand remembered his speech to Pam and Jerry North on police thoroughness. He sighed. He had been right; it could be argued that he had been too right. There were times when being the detective in charge of a murder investigation was a great deal like being a bookkeeper. You added facts instead of figures; you subtracted errors instead of debits; in the end, if you were lucky, you balanced the books. If you didn't the first time, you kept at it until you did. And people all over the country poured in facts—poured in errors along with them, and surmises. And already Inspector O'Malley felt that Weigand was keeping books badly. What O'Malley felt, he said.

The newspapers were not demanding action; big city newspapers almost never did, unless there was a political issue. Nobody had as yet found a political issue. What the newspapers were doing was to lose interest in the whole matter; *The Times* this morning had relegated it to the second front and even in the early editions of the afternoon it was below the first-page fold. Neither the district attorney nor Inspector O'Malley approved of this; the district attorney was particularly annoyed. It had been some time since his name was in the newspapers. He had pointed this out, in other words, to the commissioner, who had, without comment of his own, passed the word along to O'Mal-

ley. The commissioner had smiled faintly through
O'Malley's resultant remarks, knowing O'Malley.
O'Malley had passed the word to Weigand, not with-
out comment.

There was no point in passing the word further.
Everybody was doing very well—everybody was col-
lecting furiously. Only correlation lagged. Bill looked
at his new facts.

Dr. Merton had been traced to a small town in
Oklahoma, where he had not prospered after his wife
had divorced him; where, five years ago, he had died.
So presumably Dr. Merton was not, under another
name, in their present cast of characters; he had not
disposed of Miss Amelia Gipson when she discovered
this. Dr. Merton could be subtracted.

About Mrs. Merton there was nothing new; Washington was checking the date of her return to the
United States, if she had returned, and Washington
was slow. A police photographer, looking like a sidewalk photographer, was snapping away happily outside the apartment house in which the Burts lived,
waiting to snap Mrs. Burt. He had missed her when
she went out about ten; he was waiting for her to come
back.

Philip Spencer, Ph.D., had left Ward College in
Indiana at the end of the school year in the spring of
1942. The college was reticent, but the local police had
been insistent. There had, the college said reluctantly,
been a complaint or two about Dr. Spencer's behavior
with the students. As to the facts behind the com-
plaints, the college was non-committal; the college
clearly wished that the matter had never come up, and
seemed obscurely embarrassed. It was likely, Bill
Weigand thought, that Dr. Spencer had been sacrificed
to the laws of strict propriety. Which was what Spencer had indicated. The college flatly refused to hint at
the name of the young woman—or the young
women—involved. Weigand was not surprised.

Major Kennet Frost had been in the municipal airport in Kansas City during a good part of the afternoon
of Tuesday, September 11. He had been arguing about

his plane reservation. He had argued into the evening and then, convinced that he was not going to get the plane he wanted, had wired his wife that he would arrive in the early afternoon of the following day. He had then, unexpectedly, got on an earlier plane without, according to Western Union's records, wiring his wife of his change in plans. Presumably he had not had time. And certainly he had not been in a position to enter Amelia Gipson's apartment and poison her digestive powders. Subtract Major Kennet Frost.

John Gipson had lunched at a small restaurant in Madison Avenue on Wednesday—yesterday. But he had lunched earlier than he had indicated. Unless he had loitered over his food, he had had time to kill Florence Adams in the hotel in West Forty-second Street. The Frosts had not been identified by anybody as having lunched at Twenty-one, which meant nothing; too many people had, and far too many majors.

There was nothing new from California on the early life, courtship and marriage of the Burts. That stood as it was. No subtractions were indicated—and no additions.

Weigand smiled as he picked up the next report. Unquestionably, there was something about Pam North. Perhaps it was that, so often, her theories worked out—approximately. But her conviction that the death of Amelia Gipson was linked to some murder of the past—that there was, in a sense, murder within murder—had put somebody to work. Somebody had gone, again, into the past of Joyce Wentworth, so mysteriously and reasonlessly killed on her way home from work on a gray winter evening in 1942. It had merely meant checking old records, but old records had been checked, on Bill's own instructions. Bill's smile lingered as he read about the girl; it faded. It had been nothing to smile about; it had been cruel and incomprehensible. She had come from a little town in Indiana, leaving school to make her fortune in New York. She had—

Bill Weigand stopped suddenly. He re-read what he had just seen. She had left school, right enough. The school she had left had been Ward College. In the spring of 1942. Weigand told himself that he would be damned.

The case was full of coincidences—a good deal too full of coincidences, which were, individually, too reasonable. Here was an Indiana girl, the daughter of a sufficiently prosperous druggist; here in Indiana was a girls' school of a certain standing—of very good standing. It was natural enough she should have gone to Ward. But was it natural that Ward College should appear so frequently in the book of facts Bill Weigand was balancing? Was it merely another coincidence? Or did he want to talk, at once, with a former instructor named Philip Spencer about a beautiful girl who had, also, left Ward College in the spring of 1942, and who had been killed in December of the same year? Bill Weigand had no trouble answering the last question.

As he and Mullins went uptown in the police car, Bill considered what he had if he abandoned one tenuous theory in favor of another. He nodded to himself. He had a very interesting theory; he had a theory he could come to like.

He told Mullins as much, and Mullins shook his head, unhappily. He said what they didn't lack was theories.

"Gipson did it for money," he said. "His sister so the old girl couldn't talk. Mrs. Burt because she's really Mrs. Merton. Spencer because she got him fired *and* because she found out he'd knocked off the Wentworth dame. Or Spencer because she got him fired, period, and now he's after the Frost girl because she was the girl who got him in trouble at the college. Some guy named Hill because he thought it would be sorta fun. It's a hell of a crowded killing, loot."

"Right," Bill Weigand said, as they stopped in front of the rooming house Philip Spencer existed in. "We'll have to uncrowd it, sergeant."

Spencer was home. He was home in a little room on the street side and on the third floor; he was sitting by the only window in the room reading a book. And he called to them to come in when Weigand knocked, and he did not seem to care much who came in. He did not get up and he held his book on his lap. He wore glasses now; he looked older than he had in Weigand's office. He wore a bathrobe which could not call itself a dressing gown; although the window was part way open, the air in the room was old, much used. Philip Spencer looked up at them.

"Well," he said, "come to arrest me, lieutenant?"

"Perhaps," Weigand said. "I want to ask you some things, first."

Spencer dog-eared the corner of the page he was reading. He put the book down on the floor beside him.

"If you want to sit down, you'll have to sit on the bed," he said. "Both of you, I guess."

Weigand looked at the bed.

"So far as I've ever noticed," Spencer said, "there aren't any. Of course, I may be immune." He looked around the room with apparent interest. "I must say," he told them, "you'd expect the bed to be crawling, considering everything else."

Bill Weigand merely waited, standing.

"Why don't you say you didn't come here to talk about my bed?" Spencer asked him.

"Because I knew you would, eventually," Bill told him.

Spencer nodded. He said that was very good. He said he realized he ought to let Weigand have his chair.

"But," he said, "it's the only halfway comfortable place to sit in the room. And after all, it's my room. As E. B. White said about Rockefeller's wall. A very fine writer, incidentally."

"He is," Weigand said. "It is very incidental. When did your wife die, Mr. Spencer?"

Spencer looked at him, and there was some curiosity in his eyes. But there was none in his voice.

"November, 1942," he said.

"You took it hard," Bill said. "You still do."

It was none of his business, Spencer told him. It was

none of his described business. Spencer's voice was still unexcited, contrasting oddly with his words. It seemed like a dead voice. Bill Weigand waited.

"I am emphatic," Spencer said. "I agree. But it isn't, you know."

"I don't know," Weigand told him. "If I did, I wouldn't waste time. You took it hard."

Weigand could have it his own way, Spencer told him. He took it hard.

"What was the name of the girl who complained about you to Miss Gipson?" Weigand said. "The time you got dismissed. In the spring of 1942?"

Spencer shook his head.

"Nope," he said. "No comment."

"Was it Miss Gipson's niece?" Weigand said. "Nora Gipson? Nora Frost, now? The one you telephoned yesterday?"

"Hell no," Spencer said. "What gave you that idea?"

"Partly," Weigand told him, "the fact that you were interested enough to call her up."

Spencer shook his head, and smiled without enthusiasm. He said Weigand could call that a whim. Condolences from an old friend of the family.

"Also," he said, "I had been drinking. Naturally that may have influenced me."

"But she wasn't the girl who got you in trouble? Or who you got in trouble?" Weigand wanted to know.

The dead voice said it wished Weigand would get one thing straight.

"I didn't get any girl in trouble," he said. "Whatever you mean by it. Some nasty-minded little fool who figured any man who spoke to her was—assailing her virtue—misunderstood. Or pretended to misunderstand. For your record, it wasn't Nora Gipson."

"You knew her," Weigand told him.

Spencer agreed he knew her. He said he knew a hundred and fifty girls at Ward. He said most of them were in his classes at one time or another. He knew Nora Gipson; knew she was Amelia Gipson's niece.

"And," he said, "an attractive enough infant, from all I saw. If I had been pursuing infants."

"Which you were not," Weigand said. "Right. Who was the girl, Mr. Spencer? There's a reason I want to know."

Spencer merely shook his head. Weigand nodded. When he went on, he was merely telling a story.

"There was another pretty girl at Ward that spring," he said. "For all I know, there were hundreds. This one was thin and tall and she had red hair—I guess maybe you'd call her beautiful, not pretty. Remember a girl like that?"

Spencer did not answer, although Weigand gave him a moment. He merely waited.

"She left Ward in the spring of 1942," Weigand said. "The same time you did, Mr. Spencer. She came to New York. She got a job as a dress model—a very superior sort of dress model, in a very superior store. By the time they got through with her, she was really beautiful. She came to New York in August and got the job in October. October, 1942, that was. She also saw some talent agents and went the rounds of the producers looking for a job on the stage. She was planning a lot of things for the future."

He paused a moment and looked at Spencer. Spencer was looking out of the window. But it was evident that he was listening.

"Only," Weigand said, "she didn't have any future. Around the middle of December—December 11th, it was—somebody killed her. Somebody came up behind her on a street that wasn't very light and stuck a knife in her back. So in the end it didn't matter a damn whether she was beautiful or not." He waited a moment. "Remember a girl like that, Mr. Spencer?"

Spencer turned from the window and looked at Bill Weigand.

"There were a lot of girls at Ward," he said. "Some of them were thin and had red hair."

"Her name was Joyce Wentworth," Weigand said. "Remember her now?"

"I might," Spencer said. "I might if there were any reason to."

"Isn't there?" Weigand asked him.

"No," he said.

"Suppose," Weigand said, "there was a man like yourself, Mr. Spencer—a man who had got kicked out of a job because some girl told stories about him—stories that weren't true; weren't essentially true. Suppose that, as a result of losing this job—this man was in his forties, and trained for only one thing—the man was hard up. Suppose—"

"All right," Spencer said. "Suppose my wife died because I couldn't get her the kind of treatment she needed. Or suppose I keep feeling that that may have been the reason. Suppose she died in November, 1942, and that I took it hard. Very hard. Suppose—what with my grief, my sense of inadequacy, a kind of hopelessness that may have set in—I became somewhat unbalanced. Suppose I got to brooding about this girl—this feather-minded little fool—who had knocked hell out of my life because she was vain and silly—emotionally unstable. Or just—what word would you like, lieutenant?—avid. Suppose the girl was a thin, red-headed girl named Joyce Wentworth and I found out she was in New York and went after her. Because I was unbalanced at the time, you remember. Suppose I followed her home and stuck a knife in her. And suppose, reading about the case, Amelia Gipson remembered that Joyce Wentworth was the girl at Ward—she'd know, of course—and found out that I'd been here in New York at the time, drinking a lot and in a kind of daze, and put two and two together. Suppose she found me and told me she was going to the police. Is that the rest of your story, lieutenant?"

It could be, Weigand told him. With a postscript.

"Suppose you killed Miss Gipson to keep her from going to the police," he said.

That was obvious, Spencer said. Too obvious to need mentioning.

"Well?" Bill said, and waited.

"No," Spencer said. "As a matter of fact—no. It

was another girl; actually, I don't remember the Wentworth girl at all. There was a name in the class records—I remember that. I suppose, if I tried, I could vaguely connect it with a red-haired girl, since you suggest it. I don't remember any red-haired girl who was particularly striking."

"Were you in New York in December, 1942?" Weigand wanted to know.

Spencer shook his head.

"I was in Indianapolis," he said. He looked around the room. "In a room rather like this one. I was drunk most of the time. I wasn't dangerous to anybody. I was just—drunk."

"Can you prove it?" Weigand asked him.

"That I had a room in Indianapolis that month?" Spencer said. "I suppose so. That I didn't leave it for several days at a time—that I wasn't in New York on the eleventh—no, I don't suppose I can."

"Can you prove that the girl who accused you wasn't Joyce Wentworth?" Bill wanted to know.

Spencer hesitated a moment and then shook his head. So far as he knew, Amelia Gipson had presented the story to the head of the college in very circumspect terms. It would have been, he supposed, a Miss A who had complained. That was the method. The college president preferred not to know too much; possibly Amelia preferred not to tell too much. "For reasons of her own," he said. Except for the girl herself, he supposed there was nobody who knew the story.

"And," he said, "the girl was killed in a motor accident about a year later. One of those late-at-night, everybody-half-drunk affairs."

That, Bill told him, was inconvenient. It was very inconvenient.

"Isn't it?" Spencer said. "So I have no chance of proving my story—and the name of the girl wouldn't help, would it? Because I could just say it was any girl who got killed in that kind of an accident at about that time. I suppose there were plenty."

"Right," Bill said, "there were plenty. There are always plenty."

"But on the other hand," Spencer said, "can *you* prove anything, lieutenant? Can you prove I was in New York? That I did kill this—this Joyce Wentworth? That I also killed Amelia Gipson?"

"And Florence Adams," Weigand said. "Because if you killed one, I'd suppose you killed the others. I don't know, Mr. Spencer. I really don't know." He spoke easily, almost casually. "But if I decide you did, I can have a damn good try at it," he said, and his voice was less casual. He stood looking down at Philip Spencer and Mullins, standing a little behind him, put away his notebook. "A damn good try," he said.

Spencer looked up at him, and now he was smiling. It was difficult to interpret the smile.

"Well, lieutenant," he said, "have you decided?"

Weigand merely shook his head, and he, too, smiled.

"I'll let you know," he promised. "I'll be sure to let you know, Mr. Spencer."

It seemed to Detective Sergeant Angelo Farrichi that Lieutenant Weigand was doing it the hard way. More precisely, he was having Detective Sergeant Angelo Farrichi do it the hard way. It was a warm day, for one thing. It had been getting warmer all morning. On warm days, Sergeant Farrichi preferred a more desultory life. He also preferred not to feel silly, and snapping pictures of people walking on Park Avenue, few of whom were photographically suitable for any purpose Farrichi could think of, was unquestionably silly. Particularly when you were photographing them all on one film surface. Pushing little cards, which bore the name of a quite fictitious studio, at people who did not want them was also silly.

If you wanted pictures of people, Farrichi thought— snapping a picture of a stout woman being led down Park Avenue by a stout dog—you went and took them. If you were the police, you either went where the people were and took their pictures, or you had them brought down to the photographer's lab, where conditions were better. Usually, you photographed them behind a board with numbers on it, so that later there would be no doubt who they were. You did not pretend to be a sidewalk photographer and lie in wait.

But you did if you were a sergeant and a lieutenant told you to. Farrichi sighed and threw away a numbered card which the stout woman had seemingly not seen as he held it toward her. You did many things if you were a sergeant and a lieutenant requested it; that was the purpose of sergeants. And if you were a good detective as well as a good photographer, you did it as well as Detective Sergeant Farrichi was doing as he lay in wait for Mrs. Willard Burt.

Farrichi was the sidewalk photographer to the life. He beamed at his subjects as he maneuvered into position in front of them; he beamed as he held out the cards which were to be sent, with fifty cents, to the address given in exchange for one print of a fine action photograph. When they rejected the cards, he stopped beaming as if a switch had been thrown, threw the card away, and waited for a likely subject. Only if you had watched closely would you have noticed that the subjects Sergeant Farrichi picked were not really the most likely. Another sidewalk photographer would have noticed this and thought Farrichi very new at the game. He passed up returned soldiers walking with their girls; he ignored people obviously from out of town, pleased with themselves against the background of Park Avenue; he voided new parents with new children. You would have thought that he was concentrating on those least likely to send in their little cards, and you would have been entirely right. There was no point in making work for everybody—the work of returning money with a polite note regretting that the Eagle Photographic Studio had, overnight, gone out of business. By selecting people who would hardly care to look at themselves more frequently than was essential, Farrichi abetted the paper-saving campaign.

There was no other sidewalk photographer around to notice this, or to speculate why Farrichi chose Park Avenue in the Sixties instead of Fifth in the Forties, the traditional hunting ground. There had not been a sidewalk photographer around for several years, because of one thing and another—including a shortage both of print paper and photographers. Farrichi had wondered if this would not make people suspicious, but evidently it did not. There seemed to be a normal inclination merely to look through him.

He kept an eye on the door of the apartment house in which the Burts lived; he was never far from it. He kept in his mind Weigand's careful description of Mrs. Burt—a description so exact that it had printed a picture of her on Farrichi's sensitive, photographer's brain. He waited for her to come out, or, if she was already out, to go in. His feet hurt and his collar wilted, but his smile kept on flashing as he picked with care the most unlikely subjects for his art.

People went in and out, but none of them was Mrs. Burt. At a few minutes before eleven a very attractive young woman he had seen somewhere before came out and got into a taxicab, which started, slowed suddenly and started again.

The face puzzled Farrichi for a moment and then he placed it. She was that Mrs. North who was a friend of the lieutenant. It would be interesting to know what she was up to. A few minutes later a man came out and spoke to the doorman in a measured voice and went off in the taxicab the doorman whistled for. Farrichi had never seen him before.

It was 12:30 when another taxicab stopped in front of the apartment house. Farrichi moved up to where he could catch a glimpse of the occupant. There were two occupants, and one of them was a woman of about the right age. Farrichi moved closer and made, unconsciously, a little sound of relief. It was Mrs. Burt, all right—Mrs. Burt with a man. Oh yes, the man who had come out of the apartment house a few minutes after Mrs. North. Mr. Burt, for a guess.

Farrichi moved up and waited while Mr. Burt—assuming it was Mr. Burt—paid the driver. He waited while Mr. Burt got out and extended a hand to Mrs. Burt. Farrichi's quick fingers played with adjustments on his camera, which was a much better camera than you would have expected of a sidewalk photographer. Mrs. Burt and the man were abreast when a beaming Farrichi moved in front of them. They had slightly surprised expressions when he pressed the shutter release.

"Picture of yourselves in New York," he said, brightly, wheedlingly. "Natural pose photograph?" He beamed and held out his little card. The man with Mrs. Burt started to shake his head, and then, to Farrichi's surprise, accepted the little card. Mrs. Burt looked, Farrichi thought, slightly pained—possibly even annoyed.

"No sir," Farrichi said, heartily meaningless. "You won't make any mistake. No sir!"

Mrs. Burt and the man with her said nothing. Farrichi, beaming still, stepped aside. The two went into the apartment house. Farrichi did not look after them. He went on about his business. Between the apartment house and the nearest corner, he snapped several photographs of improbable people, one of whom abashed him by accepting the card. But at the next corner he looked at his watch, looked up at the sun, evidently decided to call it a day. He closed his camera and put it into the container swinging from his shoulder. He walked off toward the subway.

But his watch told him it was lunchtime. His stomach told him he might as well have lunch before he went in. He thought of the Villa Penza on Grand Street and of veal parmigiana and he smiled. He took the East Side subway to Grand Street and walked to the Villa Penza. The veal parmigiana was all he had expected, and the service was prompt. But Farrichi was unhurried as he ate. The lieutenant had not indicated there was any need to hurry.

Pamela North heard the telephone ringing as she fitted her key into the lock, so the key stuck. You had to push it clear in and then pull it out a little—about a sixty-fourth of an inch, Jerry had estimated—and then turn, and when you were in a hurry this was impossible. Pam pushed it in and pulled it out, but this was apparently too far. The telephone rang demandingly. Pam said "Oh!" and pushed the key in and pulled it out. She was very careful this time, and so she did not pull it out far enough.

The telephone rang.

"It'll die," Pam said. "I know it'll die. And it's probably terribly important." She wrenched at the key. The telephone rang again. It sounded to Pam as if it were getting tired.

"Wait a minute," Pam said. "Please wait a minute!" The telephone was silent. Then it rang again. Sometimes if you turned the key the wrong way and then very hard the right way it worked. "You just back up and get a running start," Pam had explained to Jerry, who had pointed out that you didn't need to if you were careful how far you pulled. Pam turned the key the wrong way and then very hard the right way and it stuck.

It's terribly important, Pam thought. It's about something happening to Jerry. He's been run over. And the hospital is trying to get me and there's only a little time. . . .

She took a deep breath to make her fingers stop trembling. She pushed the key all the way in. She counted to steady herself. "One," she said. "Two—" The telephone rang. It sounded impatient. It was giving her a last chance. "Three,"Pam said to herself, and pulled the key out a sixty-fourth of an inch. She turned it. It turned. She rushed into the apartment and dived for the telephone. It rang again as she dived. She clutched it and spoke into it. Her voice was almost a scream.

"Hello!" she screamed. "Oh, hello!"

There was no answer. They had gone away. Jerry had been run over and was dying in a hospital and she didn't know what hospital because she had gone to look at Mrs. Burt, after Jerry had almost told her not to, and Jerry was—She held the receiver off and looked at it. Then she turned it around and put the receiving end, into which she had been shouting, to her ear. She said "Hello" again, but her voice was hopeless. Then she said: *"Jerry! Darling!"*

"Hello, Pam," Jerry said. "What's the matter?"

"Are you all right, Jerry?" Pam said. "Jerry—are you all *right?*"

"Of course I'm all right," Jerry said. "Why wouldn't I be?"

"You're not run over?" Pam said. "You're not in a hospital?"

"What on earth, Pam?" Jerry said.

"You're *really* all right?" Pam said. "I mean . . . you're not hurt at all? It was you all the time?"

"What was me all the time?" Jerry said.

"The telephone?" Pam said. "It was ringing."

"Listen," Jerry said. His voice was calm, but it had a kind of desperation in it. "Of course it was ringing. You answered it. That's . . . that's how we happen to be talking on the telephone. I called you up and you heard the telephone bell ring and you answered the telephone. And it was me. See?"

"Oh," Pam said. "I know *that*. I thought it was the hospital. You see, I wasn't here."

"You . . . what?" Jerry said.

"I wasn't here," Pam said. "I mean, I'd just come back. And you'll have to say something to the management about that lock, because the key stuck and so of course I thought it was the hospital. Because the telephone was ringing."

"Oh," Jerry said. "I . . . of course. And you're all right?"

"Of course *I'm* all right," Pam said. "It was you, not me. I was all right all the time."

"Of course," Jerry said. His voice had lost its note of anxiety. "Well . . . I've recovered, darling. I called up about the funeral." He paused a moment and then spoke hurriedly. "Not mine, Pam," he said. "Amelia Gipson's. I think I ought to go . . . just as a . . . just since she . . ."

"Obviously," Pam said. "I meant to mention it this morning. Of course we have to go. Noblesse oblige."

"Well," Jerry said, "perhaps not quite that. But it

seems like a reasonably . . . thoughtful, thing to do. Don't you think?"

"Of course," Pam said. "I'll go, too."

"Well," Jerry said.

"Of course," Pam said. "We'll both be thoughtful. Only have we time for lunch first?"

The funeral, Jerry told her, was set for three o'clock. At a funeral parlor on Madison Avenue. They would have time for lunch. He suggested the Little Bar at the Ritz.

"Only of course we can't drink," Pam pointed out, agreeing to the Little Bar at the Ritz. "On account of going to a funeral." She paused, reflecting. "Maybe one each," she said. "To quiet our nerves."

Jerry said that his nerves were completely quiet.

"Well," Pam said, "they didn't sound like it. A minute ago. You sounded very puzzled and . . . perturbed, sort of." She paused a moment. "Jerry," she said. "I wish you'd take better care of yourself. You . . . you really ought to."

"I know," Jerry said. He was very grave. "Just out of the hospital, as I am."

Pam sat a moment, catching her breath, after Jerry had hung up. Then she decided she ought to tell Bill that she had not seen Mrs. Burt. She dialed; she got Bill Weigand. He was sorry she had not seen Mrs. Burt.

"I talked to Mr. Burt," she said. "I had to, because I'd pretended it was about a lost compact. That I was there, I mean. And he didn't react to the Merton case. I thought he might if he knew his wife was really Mrs. Merton."

Bill Weigand said he should have thought Burt might.

"Do you know yet, Bill?" she said, then.

"No, Pam," Bill told her. "All I've got is another possibility."

"Was it, Pam wanted to know, a good one?

"About as good as the others," Bill said. Pam said, "Oh."

"As good as mine?" she said.

Better, Bill told her. Particularly if Burt really hadn't shown interest in the Merton case.

"No more than in the others," she said. "The Joyce Wentworth case. The Purdy case. Are you going to the funeral? Because Jerry and I are, and we're having lunch at the Ritz first, and why don't you join us?"

Bill Weigand hesitated a moment. Then he agreed.

Pam sat then, duty done, and thought of things absently. She thought she must change and do her face if she was having lunch with Jerry. She jumped then, because Martini had come out from under the sofa and jumped on her. She petted the little cat abstractedly.

One thought had led to another, and the last puzzled.

"I suppose all the time I've been thinking it had to be a woman," she said, and since the little cat was in her lap now she spoke aloud. "I suppose that's it, Martini. Because of the perfume. But it could have been a man with it on for the purpose." She contemplated this and shook her head. "Or," she told Martini, "a man with an atomizer. Just to fool us."

She stroked the little cat.

"Only," she said, "it didn't stop Bill from thinking about men too. It was subconscious with me, Martini—that's mostly why I gave up Mr. Hill, probably. But I wonder why it didn't block Bill?"

It was almost the first thing she asked him when they were having their one drink around at the Ritz. He smiled at her. He said because it was only one of the little touches. He said you found them in most cases. He said they would throw you off, if you let them.

"You can be too subtle," he said. "You can be taken in by subtle things. There are half a dozen ways of explaining the perfume in Miss Gipson's room—ways that have nothing to do with Miss Gipson's killing. There are one or two ways—you've hit on one with your theory of a man with an atomizer—that might be connected with the case. Or it might actually be a woman. But the point is—it isn't important enough to stop over. Because perhaps we were supposed to stop over it. Perhaps we were supposed to think it was the significant clue. And we can't risk doing what we're supposed to do."

"But," Jerry said. "it might be important. It might really be significant."

Bill nodded. He said it might very well be.

"In which case," he said, "it will fit in as we go along—when we get on the right road. But we'll get on the right road because we find out the big things, not the little things. Because we find out who wanted to, who could have. In this case, there seem to be several people who had reason and opportunity."

"And—?" Pam said.

"And," Bill said, "we wait for a break. We do what cops always do—we put on the pressure, we wait for a break. And we keep our eyes open, so we'll see the break when it comes. Of course—the break may in itself be one of the little things. Somebody talking out of turn; somebody telling a foolish lie. Somebody having made a silly mistake. But the main thing is the pressure. The main thing is to keep the pressure on. To keep somebody feeling we're crowding him."

They finished their drinks.

"What's the new possibility?" Pam asked.

Bill told them. He said it was only a possibility. Pam said it certainly was.

"Anyway," she said, "you seem to have come around to thinking Miss Gipson was killed because of something she found out when she was reading about the old cases. As I always said."

Bill Weigand shook his head. He said he hadn't come around to thinking anything. He said he was still exploring.

"The trouble is," Pam said, "there are too many possibilities. And nothing to make any of them more than a possibility. You tell yourself a story about Mr. Spencer; I tell myself a story about Mrs. Burt. What do you tell yourselves stories about, Jerry? Sergeant Mullins?"

Jerry was very grave.

"I think Backley, the lawyer, is really Purdy, the

wife killer," he said. "I think he wasn't killed in the plane crash at all and that Miss Gipson found it out and threatened to expose him, making it necessary for him to kill her."

"Really, Jerry!" Pam said. "Really."

Jerry said it seemed as good to him as any of the others. But one eyelid drooped momentarily for Bill Weigand's benefit.

"Sergeant?" Pam said.

"The kids," Sergeant Mullins said. "The nephew and the niece, one or the other. To get the money." He contemplated. "I guess the nephew," he said. He looked at Mrs. North. "Look, Mrs. North," he said, "they can't *all* be screwy." He said it as if he were arguing with himself.

13

The afternoon newspapers, keeping the story alive
against increasing odds and bringing it up to date with
the quiet desperation known only to afternoon rewrite
men, had used the time and place of Amelia Gipson's
funeral as a lead. The results were middling; a steam
shovel would have done better, but for a funeral this
did well enough. As their cab drew up in front of the
Stuart Funeral Home, Pam looked at the people on the
sidewalk and said it looked like an opening night.

"On the contrary," Jerry told her, and paid the taxi
driver. The crowd pressed up and looked at them.

"That's the niece," a thin woman with startling
black eyes said shrilly. "That's the Frost girl."

"Naw," the man with her said. "Come on, Stella. It
ain't nobody."

"Well!" Pam said, in a soft voice to Jerry. "Well! I
hate to be such a disappointment."

There were a couple of reporters in the cleared
center of the crowd, and they looked at the Norths and
looked away again. Then the taxicab drew away and
the police car came up to the curb. The reporters
moved toward it and Bill Weigand shook his head at
them.

"Nothing yet," he said. "Sorry, boys."

"There's a rumor—" one of the boys, a tired-
looking man in his fifties, began, and Bill shook his
head a second time.

178

MURDER WITHIN MURDER   179

"No rumors," he said. "Talk to the inspector, Harry."

"Why?" said Harry, with simplicity.

"All right, Harry," Mullins said. "Break it up."

There was a man looking out the door of the Stuart Funeral Home. The door had discreet curtains not quite covering it and the man drew one of them aside. He looked worried and unhappy, and neither worry nor unhappiness sat comfortably on his face. He was not cadaverous or solemn; he was rotund and ruddy and when he opened the door he had the dignified cordiality of an automobile salesman. He raised his eyebrows at the Norths, with expectant politeness.

"North," Jerry said. "Miss Gipson's employer . . . her late employer."

"The late Miss Gipson's former employer," Mrs. North said.

The rotund man looked at her and achieved a kind of enforced gravity.

"Very sad," he said. "Very sad indeed. Chapel A, if you please."

He looked past the Norths at Weigand and for a moment he was doubtful. He saw Mullins, and doubt vanished.

"Is it necessary?" he said, in a hurt voice. "Is it really necessary, inspector?"

"What?" Weigand said.

"This crowd," the man said, waving at it. "This— notoriety. The police." He sighed. "Everything," he said.

"I'm afraid so," Weigand told him. "It won't last, you know."

"Sad," the man said. "Very sad. Chapel A."

The reception-room was very restrained and somewhat dark. There was a dignified hush about it and a faint smell of flowers. There was organ music faintly in the air, as if an organ were being played in the next block. The chairs in the room were austere, as if they meant to discourage relaxation and provide comfort grudgingly, but they were upholstered in heavy, dark brocades. The Stuart Funeral Home did not discourage thought of the dead by pampering the living. But it did not forget that the living paid the bills, and wanted something for their money.

There were three doors leading from the reception-room and there were dimly illuminated signs over them. Like exit signs in theaters, only a sort of purple, Mrs. North thought. One sign said "Chapel A" and another "Chapel B." The third said "Office." Pam North looked through the door marked "Office"—the other two doors were closed by hangings—and saw a corridor leading away from the street. Off one side of the corner there was a wide arch, leading to another room. She could not see what was in the other room. The Norths, with Weigand and Mullins following them, went to the door marked "Chapel A." Jerry reached around Pam and drew back the curtain for her.

The room was much dimmer than the reception-room, and was constructed like a small church. There were pews, facing a wall heavily draped with velvet. The velvet seemed to glow dimly with purple light. The sound of the organ music was more perceptible; the organ might now be as close as the next building. There was nobody in the room but, as they entered, the organ music increased perceptibly in volume.

It was a room to whisper in, and Pam whispered.

"Somebody looks through the curtains," she said. As she spoke the room slowly became lighter, although there was no obvious identification of the source of light. It was still a kind of purplish light; a light which was a more revealing kind of darkness. The increased light seemed to focus, in a mood of almost overpowering reverence, on a coffin placed on a draped pedestal in front of the curtains at the end of the chapel. There were flowers around it, and over it.

"The poor thing," Pam said. "Would she have liked this, Jerry?"

"I don't know," he said. "I shouldn't think so. But I suppose it's inevitable."

"We're early," Pam said. She still whispered. "What time is it, Jerry?"

"Ten of three," he told her.

"I wish it weren't so dark," Pam said. She thought a moment. "I wish it weren't so—real," she said. "And—so unreal, at the same time."

Jerry said he knew. He touched her arm and they went to the rear pew on the right. Weigand and Mullins, who seemed to have been delayed in the reception-room, came in and Bill sat down on the opposite side of the aisle. Mullins stood against the rear wall, and the wall seemed to swallow him. The organ music swelled a little and Mr. and Mrs. Burt came in. Mrs. Burt was crying a little and Mr. Burt's hand was protectingly on her arm. When she saw the casket, Mrs. Burt made a sound like a tiny sob.

"There, my dear," Mr. Burt said. "There."

They sat down in front of the Norths. Mr. Burt saw Mrs. North in the gloom and bowed with dignity and restraint, as befitted the surroundings. The Burts sat decorously. Three women came in whom Mrs. North had, as well as she could tell in the light provided, never seen before. They looked at the flower-covered coffin and one of them dabbed her eyes with a handkerchief and they sat down. Pam looked across at Bill Weigand and he shook his head. He shook it again when another middle-aged couple entered. These were newcomers, Pam thought; Amelia Gipson had had more friends than they had found. Then the manager of the Holborn Annex came in, looking very sad and grave, and after him a tiny, fluttery woman who was probably, Pam thought, the hostess of that tea room at which Miss Gipson had so often eaten. She looked, at any rate, like the hostess of a tea shop. Then a man came in by himself and looked around and sat down next to Jerry. Even through the heavy fragrance of the flowers, Mrs. North detected a fragrance which was, she decided, gin. If Mr. Spencer had really come, this should be Mr. Spencer. She looked across at Bill and formed the name "Spencer" with her lips. Bill looked puzzled a moment. Then he nodded. The music came up then and the curtains at the end of the chapel were held aside by a white hand and Nora Frost came into the room, with her brother behind her. She was in black. John Gipson wore a black armband. They both wore grave, detached expressions. Major Frost came in after his brother-in-law and he looked as if he wished he were somewhere else. The music swelled and, behind Major Frost, a man who could only be a clergyman came into the room. The white hand let the curtains fall back, then.

The music continued as the Frosts and John Gipson sat down in one of the front pews. It continued as the clergyman moved around the coffin and stood in front of it. He stood there, gravely, unhurried, and the music faded and died away.

"Let us pray," the clergyman said.

Detective Sergeant Angelo Farrichi finished his coffee, sighed comfortably and looked at his watch. It was almost two o'clock. Reluctantly, he pushed his chair back, and contentedly tasting coffee, red wine and, under them, veal parmigiana, he went toward the street. Passing, he slapped the proprietor on the back; outside he paused and lighted a cigarette. He strolled toward headquarters. But as he entered the building he ceased to stroll; he became the alert detective returning with the spoils. He went to the photolab.

"And what are you made up as?" the lab technician asked him, looking at him with amusement. Farrichi's sense of peace was not disturbed. He waved at the technician and went into a darkroom. He got to work, not hurrying. He found he had something; he made a contact print. It was pretty good for that kind of job. He put the print in the dryer and went to a telephone. He asked for Lieutenant Weigand and got Weigand's office. He got Stein.

"Well," Farrichi said, "I got the Burts. How many prints does the loot want?"

"Where the hell have you been, Farrichi?" Stein wanted to know.

"Listen," Farrichi said, his sense of peace diminishing. "It took time to get them. The way the loot wanted it done. How many prints does he want?"

Farrichi had better ask him, Stein said. If he were

Farrichi he would go and ask him, taking the print he had. He told Farrichi that Weigand was at the funeral.

"Listen," Farrichi said, "is he in a hurry, Bennie?"

"I don't know," Stein said. "But if I were you, I'd be in a hurry. He might like it. He won't not like it. See?"

Farrichi saw. He wangled a car on the plea of emergency. It took him almost half an hour, all told, to get the car and get, in it, to the Stuart Funeral Home. It was 3:20 when he got there. The crowd was still outside; it looked at him with mild interest. The rotund man at the door looked at him with mild interest and it was not noticeably enhanced when Farrichi asked for Lieutenant Weigand.

"Inside," the rotund man said. "The Service is almost over. It would be better if you waited here."

Farrichi sat down. The rotund man went back to the door. It was a hell of a dismal place, Farrichi thought; the darkroom was cheerful by comparison. He'd just as soon give the print to Weigand and get along. He got up and walked over to Chapel A, from which reverent sounds were coming. He started in and bumped into Mullins standing just inside the door. He pushed an envelope containing the print into Mullins' hand, said "For the loot, ask him how many prints he wants," and backed out. Mullins came out after him, opening the envelope. He peered at the photograph in the half light, holding it this way and that. Then he looked around, saw the door marked Office, and went through it, beckoning Farrichi to follow him.

". . . an exemplary life," the clergyman was saying, "devoted to that most sacred duty—instruction of the young—the opening to them of the doors of light. In her life, Amelia Gibson" . . . the "B" was very clear in his excellent diction, but Amelia Gipson could not hear it; could not correct it . . . "gave to all of us an example of consecration, of devotion. She . . ."

It was hard to listen to. It was sincere, it was worthy. Some of it was true. It was not Amelia Gipson as she had been; it was Amelia Gipson as an abstraction. But some of it was true. She had taught. Perhaps she had opened to some of those she taught a door that led to light. If there was a doubt, she deserved the benefit of it. But it was hard to listen to.

Pam North stopped listening. She watched the backs of heads, wondering what went on inside the heads. She looked at the back of Helen Burt's head, and wondered if she were thinking—now—that she had caused all this; if now she were thinking that she would give anything she might ever have to have this thing undone. She looked at the back of Willard Burt's head, and wondered who he reminded her of when he spoke; she looked at Bill Weigand's profile, dim on the other side of the aisle, and wondered if he really knew, or had guessed—or had a hunch. She looked at the back of a dignified male head two rows in front of Weigand and wondered if he were Mr. Backley, the lawyer, because he looked as a lawyer named Backley ought to look, and then she looked at Jerry and smiled faintly as she thought of the theory to which Jerry had pretended. Mr. Backley, indeed. Mr. Purdy indeed—

Because Mr. Purdy was—

The man beyond Jerry stood up. He stood up and swayed a little, and he spoke in a voice which was neither hushed nor reverent. He spoke in a harsh, strained voice, and very rapidly.

"This is an outrage," he said. "This · unbearable. Sir, you are insulting every teacher who ever tried to bring a glimmer of intelligence into the head of some forsaken brat. Amelia Gipson was—"

Everything stopped. The clergyman stopped; there was in the room a kind of startled stillness; it was as if the room gasped.

"She was a liar," the man said. He almost shouted it. "She hurt everybody she could reach. She was a vicious—a vicious, poisonous hag. She. . . ."

Bill Weigand was standing up. Men moved toward the speaking man from the shadows, men Pam North had not seen in the shadows. Bill Weigand spoke and his voice was level and hard.

"Sit down, Spencer," he said. "Sit down."

Philip Spencer did not sit down. He turned toward Weigand.

"The policeman," he said. "The ever-present policeman. The upholder of propriety; the seeker out of the evil doer. Lieutenant whatever your name is, you make me sick." He looked around. "You all make me sick," he said. "A bunch of sniveling—"

One of the men who had come out of the shadows reached Philip Spencer. He took hold of him roughly, and pulled him out into the aisle.

"Sniveling fools, whining over a lying—" Spencer said, and the detective who had him clapped a hard hand over Spencer's mouth. And Philip Spencer went out of Chapel A very abruptly, as if he had suddenly flown into the air. The clergyman stood with his mouth open, looking at the backs of heads. Then the heads turned and all the eyes focused on the clergyman, as if he now would do something to justify this affront. He kept his mouth open for a moment. Then he spoke.

"I deeply regret this unseemly . . ." he said.

Pam North didn't doubt his regret; Philip Spencer had been unseemly enough. She whispered to Jerry.

"He was drunk, wasn't he?" she said. "Or crazy?"

"Drunk," Jerry whispered. "Very. Maybe crazy, too."

The clergyman was obviously unsettled. He looked at his audience with what seemed to be reproach; he moved just perceptibly away from the coffin, as if he held its quiet occupant in some way responsible for this flouting of decency and interruption of remarks. He looked at some notes, and apparently had difficulty reading them. He abandoned eulogy, and turned to the prayer book.

Pam listened then, to sad and beautiful words, but she listened uneasily. Her nerves tingled, as if something else were going to happen. They still tingled, as the clergyman finished and the organ began again, very soft at first, swelling slowly. The clergyman held up a hand of benediction as the music swelled.

Bill Weigand seemed to have gone, very quietly, from his seat. She wondered if he was arresting Philip

Spencer. Would it be for disturbing the peace? But the only peace that mattered—the only peace in the room which was real and quiet—had not been disturbed. Amelia Gipson had not heard the voice of drunken hatred which upbraided her.

Bill Weigand looked at Philip Spencer with distaste. Spencer looked back at him, and there was still anger in his eyes.

"All right," Spencer said, "it made me sick . . . the whole thing. So . . . I created a disturbance."

"Drunk and disorderly," Bill said. The man who held Spencer by the arm nodded. Bill looked at Spencer. "And I may as well tell you," he said, "I'll try to get you sent to Bellevue for observation."

"Much good it will do you," Spencer said.

Bill said it might do good.

"Obviously," he said, "you've very little control over yourself, Mr. Spencer. Obviously, you're . . . possessed by your hatred of Amelia Gipson. Where were you Tuesday afternoon, say? Was it a cunning hatred then . . . and did you pull this to make us think you're only an emotional, harmless drunk?"

Spencer asked him what he thought. He was surly.

"I think I'd like to have the doctors look you over," Weigand said. "Take him along and get him booked."

He turned away, heading back toward the door of Chapel A, in which there was now a stir of movement. But Mullins came through the door from the office and Mullins' voice stopped the movement. Mullins' voice was low—Mullins did not easily ignore a religious atmosphere—but it was urgent.

"Loot!" Mullins said. "Come here. I want to show you something."

Mullins led Weigand back along the corridor which led to the office, and Mullins was moving fast. The office was not funereal; the office was bright and businesslike. Mullins had a photograph flat on a desk, under a light. He pointed at it.

Weigand looked. Farrichi had done an O.K. job. But it was only a picture of Mr. and Mrs. Willard Burt, getting out of a taxicab; only of the Burts and the man who drove the taxi. Bill Weigand looked enquiringly at Mullins.

"Loot," Mullins said, "you know I never forget a face. Right?"

"Sometimes you do," Weigand said. "Mostly you don't. Well?"

Mullins pointed. Weigand followed his finger. He looked at Mullins.

"You know who that is?" Mullins asked, and there was triumph in his voice.

Weigand looked again. He looked back at Mullins again.

"Let's have it, sergeant," Weigand said, and now his voice was crisp.

Mullins let him have it. When Bill looked at him he nodded.

"Hell yes,"he said. "I worked on it. I never forget a case, loot."

They went fast down the corridor to the reception-room. Jerry North was standing in it, obviously waiting. They went past him into Chapel A, and came out almost at once.

"They're gone," Jerry told him. "Where's Pam?" He did not sound worried.

"It isn't Pam . . ." Bill began, and then stopped. "I thought she was with you, naturally," he said.

Jerry shook his head. He said some people from the office had stopped him and, when he turned back, Pam had gone.

"So had you and Mullins," he said. "I supposed she was with you." And now there was a note of uneasiness in Jerry North's voice. The uneasiness grew among the three of them as they looked at one another. It was very real by the time they had made a quick search of the funeral home and found no Pamela North anywhere in it.

But the rotund doorman had some news. They identified Pamela for him, and after a moment he nodded.

"She went out a couple of minutes ago," he said.

"With an older woman. I guess she got in a cab with her. Anyway, they were headed for a cab."

There was a moment when the funeral service ended when Pamela North found herself alone. Some people from Jerry's office had come to the funeral—to pay respect to a former colleague and also, Pam thought, to get an afternoon off—and one of them had called to Jerry and Jerry had turned to speak to them. Bill had gone out and apparently Mullins was with him. Pam turned to join Jerry and the little group from the office and then Helen Burt was beside her. Helen Burt was small, almost wispy, in the scented gloom and she put her fingers on Pamela North's arm. The fingers were trembling. Pam turned.

"Oh, my dear," Helen Burt said. "My dear Mrs. North. Can you—a moment?"

Pam looked at Mrs. Burt, who was very excited, very keyed up.

"Mrs. Burt," Pam said. "Yes?"

"I want to tell you," Mrs. Burt said. "Then you can tell your husband—the detective. I see now I can—all the time I've wanted to. Oh, all the time."

She was not very coherent. Her words came whispered, rushing from her mouth. She kept her fingers on Pam's arm. She was like a frightened person, but Pam did not think she was frightened.

"About the letter," Helen Burt said. "I realize now I can. It was what that dreadful man said—such a dreadful thing to say. But then I realized it was really true."

"What was true?" Pam said. "What did you realize, Mrs. Burt?" Pam's own voice was low; hardly more than a whisper.

"That poor dear Amelia didn't—didn't tell the truth," Helen Burt said. "That she was—that she lied about people. To hurt them. That that was what she had done to us. I knew it—I knew it had to be that way. Of course. But it was his saying it that—that—"

"That made you really feel it was true," Pam said,

when Helen Burt seemed lost. "Made you really convinced?"

"That was it," Mrs. Burt said. "And then I knew I had to tell you so that you could tell your husband. Because it isn't right that anything should be kept from him. Is it, dear?"

"Jerry isn't—" Pam began, and then she stopped. If Mrs. Burt had something to tell which was as important as Mrs. Burt seemed to feel it was, it didn't matter whether she was confused about Jerry. Apparently she thought Jerry was the detective, not Bill. But it would work out the same.

"Is it about the letter?" Pam said. "The letter you wrote Miss Gipson?"

Helen Burt looked at her and seemed surprised.

"Oh, of course, my dear," she said. "I thought you understood that."

Apparently Helen Burt thought she had explained what she had not explained. But that didn't matter either.

"You want to tell me about the letter," Pam said. "About why you really wrote it?"

"So you can tell your husband," Helen Burt said.

"Why me?" Pam said. "Why just me? Why not—oh, just tell my husband?"

Helen Burt shook her head.

"I couldn't," she said. "I couldn't make him see. A man wouldn't understand."

At the present rate, Pam thought, she was not going to understand either. Mrs. Burt was, she thought, very close to hysteria. Or was she supposed to think that Mrs. Burt was very close to hysteria? Was all of this—this nervous fluttering about the center of something, this emotional overcharge—something being done for her benefit, for some reason not immediately guessable? Pam tried to cut through the strange excitement which surrounded the older woman.

"Of course," Pam said. "Of course I'll be glad to have you tell me whatever you want to, Mrs. Burt. What—"

Mrs. Burt shook her head.

"Not here," she said. "Come to the apartment with me. Willard's gone by his office and there will be just the two of us. Oh, please, Mrs. North!"

"Well," Pam said, hesitating a little. "I'll tell Jerry. Because he'd worry if I just disappeared, you know."

Mrs. Burt shook her head. Her fingers gripped Pam's arm.

"No, dear," she said. "You mustn't. He . . . he'll insist on coming too. He'll make me tell it his way. Not my way." She looked at Pam intently. "It has to be my way," she said. "Just this once, my dear. You have to help me."

She seemed to try to read Pam's face. When she did not read what she wanted to find there, her fingers loosened on Pam's arm.

"I thought you would," she said, and her voice had lost confidence. It seemed to Pam that Mrs. Burt was like a child who had been denied something it had counted on, and could not understand why. It also occurred to Pam that Mrs. Burt was unpredictable; that she fluttered on the surface of her own changing feelings, and that whatever she had to tell might have to be told now.

"Of course I will," Pam said. "I'll go with you. Of course."

Gently, Pam North turned the older woman toward the door. Then, as she began to walk after her, she looked back quickly at Jerry, planning to call his name softly. But he was looking at her and she made gestures instead of speaking. She gestured toward Mrs. Burt, and toward herself, and pointed out through the door, and made with her lips, soundlessly, the words "she wants to talk." She made the words very carefully and she was sure Jerry would be able to read her lips, because he so often could.

She turned and went after Mrs. Burt when she had finished this pantomime, and it was not until she was on the sidewalk that the thought came to her that Jerry had been very unresponsive. She was in a cab with Mrs. Burt before it occurred to her that the reason Jerry had been unresponsive might well be that he had not seen her at all, but had been looking out at nothing over the heads of people who bored him. Because Jerry did that too, and you could never tell whether he saw you or not.

"Of course he did," Pam reassured herself. "Of course he did." And anyway, she thought, there was nothing to do about it now.

"You see, my dear," Helen Burt said, "I knew it couldn't be true, but I had always trusted Amelia. She was so different when she was a girl—when we were both girls. It's hard to realize that people have changed. It wasn't until that man called her all those things—those dreadful things—that I really realized that she had—oh, made it all up."

She paused and looked at Mrs. North.

"How could she, my dear?" she said. "Why would she want to?"

"But Mrs. Burt," Pam said, "I don't know what she did."

Mrs. Burt smiled. Now that she had Pam in the cab with her, now that her plan—whatever it was—was developing as she wished, she seemed much calmer.

"I know, dear," she said. "I'm terribly excited. It's . . . it's the relief, I suppose. I hadn't realized how much . . . how close I came really to believing what she said."

Even though calmer she was still incoherent, Pam thought, and wished people would say what they meant. As, Pam thought, I always do.

"What did she say?" Pam asked, saying what she meant.

But Mrs. Burt shook her head, and then moved it slightly to indicate the taxicab driver. Then she shook it again.

"All right," Pam said.

"It was a beautiful service," Mrs. Burt said. "In spite of everything. Didn't you think so, my dear? So . . . suitable. And Dr. Malcolm is always so fine."

"The clergyman?" Pam said. "Is he?"

"Always," Mrs. Burt said. "Oh, always."

"Well," Pam said, "that's nice."

The subject seemed to be exhausted. But, fortunately, the trip was short. The cab swung into the curb and a doorman opened the door. He was an aged doorman; heavy with respectability. And in the apartment house, cavernous respectability surrounded them; creaking respectability bore them aloft to the Burt apartment. Mrs. Burt unlocked the door to the apartment and fluttered less as she led Pam North toward the living-room.

"Isn't this nice?" she said vaguely. "Shall we have a cup of tea?"

Pam shook her head.

"I mustn't," she said. "I must hurry back, you know. Because nobody knows where I am. Or maybe they don't."

Mrs. Burt nodded and said, "Oh, of course. I'm afraid it was terribly selfish of me. But as soon as I heard that awful man, everything was clear and I knew what I had to do. I had to tell somebody about the letter and then I saw you and I said, 'Mrs. North will understand,' and I'm afraid I really didn't think about your plans. Wasn't that dreadful of me, my dear?"

Pam shook her head and said it was all right. But then she waited, and her attitude was calculated to bring Mrs. Burt to whatever point she was drifting toward.

"Anyway," Mrs. Burt said, "the maid is off this afternoon and I let the cook go too, so I don't suppose we could have tea."

"About the letter you wrote Miss Gipson," Pam said. "About whatever lies she told you. That you thought were merely mistakes."

"Of course," Mrs. Burt said, "I always knew what she said couldn't be true. Simply couldn't. But . . . I was still afraid. You know how it is, my dear?"

"Yes," Pam said, "what did she accuse you of, Mrs. Merton?"

"Mrs. Burt looked at her strangely.

"Merton?" she repeated. She seemed very puzzled.

"I'm sorry," Pam said. "I mispoke myself, Mrs. Burt."

"Oh," Mrs. Burt said. "Yes. Didn't you ask about a Mrs. Merton once before, Mrs. North?"

"Did I?" Pam said. "I don't remember. It doesn't matter, does it?"

"Of course not," Mrs. Burt said. "I never knew anybody named Merton, Mrs. North."

"All right," Pam said. "What did she accuse you of, Mrs. Burt?"

"Accuse me of?" Mrs. Burt said. "Oh, you're thinking of what I said the letter was about. But I'm afraid that wasn't true. She didn't accuse me of anything. It was about . . . Willard. Mr. Burt, you know."

"*Mr.* Burt?" Pam said, more or less involuntarily. Mrs. Burt looked at her in surprise and said, oh, of course Mr. Burt.

"A dreadful thing," she said. "That he was planning to kill me. To get my money. A dreadful . . . cruel . . . oh, a terrible thing."

"That Mr. Burt was?" Pam said. "Planning to kill you?" It sounded fatuous, her repetition. But Pam North felt fatuous. She felt completely and disturbingly confused.

"With poison," Mrs. Burt said. "It was a mad, awful thing for her to say. She said he had done it before."

"But," Pam said, "you'd have not—I mean—well, obviously he hadn't." She thought a moment. "You mean other women?" she said. "Other wives? Had he been married before?"

"Oh yes," Mrs. Burt said. "Of course, dear. So had I. His wife died. He told me all about it. But Amelia said he had poisoned his other wife. She said perhaps more than one, but one she was sure of. She said he was supposed to be dead; that he was supposed to have been killed in—"

It clicked, then—suddenly and frighteningly.

"Mr. Purdy!" Pam said. "She said he was a man named Purdy!"

But Mrs. Burt did not answer. She was looking across the room, and her eyes were widening and something seemed to be happening to her face.

"Why don't you answer her, my dear?" Willard Burt said, from the doorway in which he was standing. "Was that what your dear Amelia told you?"

But it was not his presence, or his innocuous words which caused the strange thing to happen to Mrs. Burt's face. Pam realized this as she, too, looked at Mr. Burt. It was the fact that he was carrying a gun. He was carrying it quite openly.

"Why don't you answer her, my dear?" Mr. Burt said again, and he came on into the room. The little gun—a very small gun, really, Pam thought—was partly lifted at his side. It was ready.

Pam looked at Mrs. Burt, and what she saw was horrible. Because, in a second, Mrs. Burt had learned that Amelia Gipson had not lied. And Helen Burt made a little sound in her throat; a tiny, whimpering sound.

Pamela North looked away from Helen Burt—looked away hurriedly. It was better to look at Mr. Burt, whose face had not changed so. It was better to look at Mr. Burt, even when he was carrying a gun. And Pam spoke, saying without consideration something she now suddenly remembered.

"That was how you knew," she said. "About the roaches. About there not being any."

The quiet little gray man who had been calling himself Willard Burt nodded gravely.

"It was a slip," he said. "I realized only later that I wasn't supposed to know—that no outsider was supposed to know. I remembered the police had kept that a secret. They didn't even tell me, but of course they didn't need to. I worked it out. No roaches. Hence, why roach poison? It was then I decided to run for it, of course."

His voice was very slow and careful; even slower than it had been before. Hearing it now, with her new knowledge, Pam remembered whose voice it was like. It was, in its deliberation only, like a voice all the world had listened to—and heard grow stronger and more sure during the years, but not less deliberate.

"You used to stammer," Pam said. "You cured yourself of it. By talking very slowly."

Burt nodded. He said she was very shrewd.

"Unfortunately for you," he said then, "you were not shrewd enough. You didn't really appreciate my slip this morning—not in time. But probably you would have. Eventually. Only as things have turned out, it doesn't matter, does it?"

Helen Burt spoke then. She spoke with an effort, dully.

"You were going to kill me," she said. "To get my money. It was . . . *it was why you married me.*"

She was telling a dreadful truth to herself.

Burt merely looked at her. He seemed to be smiling.

"That was what Amelia said," Mrs. Burt said. "She said you were Purdy . . . she said everything fitted. She said . . ." Helen Burt stopped and sat, looking at nothing.

"Go on, my dear," Willard Burt said, in his slow voice. "What did she say? I wondered. When she talked to me she was not—explicit."

"She went to you?" Pam said. "As well as to . . . to Mrs. Burt?"

Burt nodded.

"Of course I laughed at her," he said. "I tried to make it seem absurd to her. But she still said she was going to the police. And naturally, I couldn't let her do that."

"Naturally," Pam said.

"Because," Burt said, "although I was never actually booked, you know, I was quite sure they would have my fingerprints. Quite sure. Don't you think they would have, Mrs. North?"

He waved the little gun at her.

"Yes, Mr. Burt," she said, and she looked at the little gun. "Yes, I think they have your prints. I don't think you'll get away with anything."

Burt smiled at that, and came across the room and sat down facing them.

"Don't you, Mrs. North?" he said, and his voice held polite enquiry. "Why?"

Pam thought there had never been a single word spoken—a single innocent word—which had so dreadful a finality as Mr. Burt's politely enquiring "why?"

Jerry North and Weigand looked at each other and at the doorman.

"With an older woman," the doorman repeated. He considered. "She seemed very much cut up, the older woman did. Friend of the deceased. Very sad."

He smiled at them, a sad smile which pointedly accepted the transitory nature of human life.

"Mrs. Burt?" Jerry said to Bill, and his voice was quick and worried. His eyes demanded information from Bill Weigand. "Was Pam right after—" he began, but Bill cut in. He shook his head, almost impatiently.

"Was a man with them?" he asked the doorman. "A middle-aged man, about average height, gray hair? Very quiet in manner?"

The doorman shook his head.

"Just the two of them," he said. He thought about it. "There was a man like that around," he said. "But he went out later—several minutes later. He got a taxicab."

Bill Weigand turned to Jerry and his expression was tentatively reassuring.

"Burt," he said. "As long as he wasn't with them—" His tone finished it. Jerry looked at him and said he'd be damned.

"For Burt," Weigand said, "read Purdy. Who used sodium fluoride on his wife. Who wasn't killed in a plane accident after all. Or so Mullins says."

"How—?" Jerry said, and then moved after Weigand, who was on his way. Mullins answered from behind Jerry.

"Picture," Mullins said. "Like the lieutenant says, I never forget a face. Don't you, loot?"

Weigand was ahead of them, moving toward the police car parked at the curb. He did not answer.

"Anyway," Mullins said, as they hurried, "that's

what the loot says. That I never forget a face. And I worked on the Purdy case." He held the car door open for Jerry North. "A little, anyhow," he said. "So when I saw the picture of the Burts—the one the loot had taken—I knew the guy was Purdy."

Weigand started the car with a jerk. He headed uptown.

"Their apartment?" Jerry said, guessing.

Weigand said "yes" without turning his head. When traffic halted at the next corner, he touched the siren and they went around it.

"Apparently," Weigand said, still not looking around, "Mrs. Burt has decided to talk. And I don't think her husband will like it." He turned right. "Or the person she talks to," he said. He went across the down lane of Park Avenue with his siren growling and turned north. Jerry North leaned forward in the rear seat, urging the car on.

It was very still in the Burts' living-room after the man they had been calling Willard Burt asked his question. They were three people sitting at their ease in a handsome room, furnished with dignity. Murder had never come more quietly into a room, nor behaved in better taste.

Neither woman spoke, so after a polite pause, Mr. Burt continued.

"You see, Mrs. North," he said, "there will be no cause to suspect me of anything. It will be a clear case of murder and suicide. You will have discovered that my dear wife killed Amelia Gipson and will have charged her with it—very incautiously, of course. But then—you are not a very cautious person, are you, Mrs. North? And she, being trapped, will shoot you and then herself. Emotional, of course—not really a logical thing to do. But then you are not very logical, are you, my dear?"

He waited for one of them to say something, but they both merely looked at him. Pam's eyes were quick and frightened, but very alert. Helen Burt's eyes seemed to see nothing.

"I will come in somewhat later and find you both," he said. "Through the front door this time. Not by the service entrance. I will be very shocked, of course—very grieved."

"You won't get away with it," Pam told him. "You're—you're crazy, you know."

Willard Burt looked a little surprised; almost hurt. He shook his head.

"You have very conventional views, my dear Mrs. North," he told her. "Very—limited views. I am not in the least crazy. I am very logical. I have always been very logical. My dear wife is really quite wealthy, you know."

He's willing to talk, Pam thought. He really is a little crazy; he wants to boast. If I can stall him—She looked quickly, trying not to seem to look, at the objects near her—at a metal lamp on the table by which she was sitting; at a glass ashtray.

"It really wouldn't work, Mrs. North," the gray man said. "By the time you picked anything up, you would be dead. Don't you know that? Bullets travel so rapidly, Mrs. North."

Pam North did not answer. She did not seem to hear.

"Miss Gipson worked it out," she said. "You weren't so good after all. Were you?"

He smiled at that. He said it was chance. He said there was always room for chance.

"I was rather completely described before," he said. "In the newspapers. There are some things it is quite impossible to change, of course. And Amelia had—such a suspicious mind, didn't she, Helen? She thought I was after your money first, didn't she, my dear? And then she noticed things—the way I spoke, that I was the right age; that—"

Mrs. Burt interrupted. She spoke dully.

"She said the methods were the same," she said. "All the way from the time we met. But it was when I happened to mention to her what he'd said about the roaches that—that she told me. Of course, she never knew—not really knew. She didn't pretend to. But she wanted me to hire a detective to find out."

The gray man looked at her and his eyebrows drew together.

"The roaches, my dear?" he said. "I don't understand." He paused. Then—and it was an inconceivable thing to Pam, watching him—he reddened a little. He's embarassed, Pam thought. He's actually embarrassed!

"Oh," he said. "I remember now."

"He saw roaches in the apartment," Mrs. Burt said. "But nobody else saw them. And he said we'd have—"

Pam was nodding.

"Have to get some roach poison, didn't he?" she said. She looked at the gray man. "You were really a fool, weren't you?" she said. "So—childish. Making the same mistake twice."

He was annoyed. And that he should be annoyed—angry—was mad—coldly, horribly mad. As she looked at him now, Pam felt herself begin to tremble. Because now he was lifting the little gun.

He started to speak, and instead of words there was a kind of scraping sound in his mouth; he tried to speak and his lips, his whole face contorted.

"Duh-duh-duh-d," he said, and then stopped and tried again. "Duh-duh—" He made it. "Don't say that, you—" he said, getting the words out through his stammer. "Duh-duh-don't—"

He stopped and seemed to steady himself and then he spoke, very slowly—very carefully—without a stammer.

"I abandoned that, of course," he said. "I had another method for my dear wife; I realized I was repeating myself. But for Amelia—there was so little time, you see."

He was explaining it. He was telling them that he was really a very good murderer. It should have been funny. And it was horrible.

And as he explained—as he justified himself—he lowered the little gun again, although still it was ready.

"Amelia hurried me," he said. "She shouldn't have hurried me. And the little fool who let me have her key—she tried to hurry me, too." He paused and looked at Pamela North. He spoke even more slowly than before. "I don't allow myself to be hurried, Mrs. North," he said. "Not by anyone. You have tried to hurry me, Mrs. North."

And now the gun came up again and, as she saw it rising, Pam threw herself from the chair and, as she dived toward the floor, clutched at the heavy glass ashtray. Her fingers touched it and writhed for a hold, and the smooth glass evaded them as if it were alive. And then she heard a gun. And then everything was black.

14

Pamela North's head ached and there was a large bump just at the hairline on her forehead. She looked at Jerry and Bill Weigand, sitting comfortably where they could look at her as she lay on the sofa, and their expressions of gentle commiseration did not appeal to her.

"All right," she said, "I knocked myself out by diving into the leg of the table. All right. But anyway, I was there."

"Of course, Pam," Jerry said.

"And," Pam said, "I was warm. Which was as much as any of us were. Except poor Amelia, of course." She reached up and stroked the tiny cat which lay on her shoulder. "We were all stupid, weren't we, Martini?" she said. "And they were as stupid as anyone." She considered. "More," she said. "Anyway—I got the right family. And the right idea." She paused again. "Underlying, of course," she said.

"We were all there, finally," Bill Weigand told her. "I don't pretend to be proud of it—if any of it. But we did get there."

"The United States Cavalry," Pam said. "Mullins to the rescue. With his trusty automatic."

Bill Weigand was equable about that.

"Better late than and so forth," he said. "Mullins did save your life. And Mullins never forgets a face. Which was what started the cavalry."

Pam smiled, then.

"Dear Mullins," she said. "I'm appreciative, Bill. Only my head does ache. And Mullins hit just his hand?"

"Just his hand," Bill agreed. "And the gun more than the hand. He just needed a bit of—wrapping up. We wrapped him up. He's been talking ever since, by the way. Seems very anxious to explain himself. Feels that it was very unfair things didn't work out better. Keeps saying he got hurried toward the end, and that he can't bear to be hurried."

"Because he stammers," Pam said. "Don't bite ears, Martini. When he's hurried he stammers, and that embarrasses him. It's—it's a kind of phobia. Is he crazy, Bill?"

Bill Weigand shook his head. He said no crazier than most murderers. Rather businesslike, on the whole, although with a tendency to slip up. He'd fooled them nicely on the crash business, for example—he, and a lot of luck. He had had an hour's layover in Kansas City when he was trying to fly out of reach; he had found a man who, for a hundred dollars, would take his place in the plane, answering to his name and all. So that the police would keep chasing him on across the country while he turned south and holed in. Which would have confused them, even without the crash, in which the substitute was burned to death—and to unrecognizability.

"You'd think, to hear him talk, that he planned the crash too," Bill said. "He likes to think he's a great planner. When his luck is good, that is. Miss Gipson's identification of him was just bad luck, of course."

"Which it was, after all," Jerry North said.

"Right," Bill agreed. "Sheer bad luck. As long as nobody suspected him, he was all right. But if any suspicion started an enquiry—even if the suspicion was wrong; even if somebody thought he was Judge Crater—he was out of luck. Because, of course, we'd picked up Purdy's fingerprints, just as he thought."

There was a little pause. Jerry and Bill had drinks beside them, and both drank. Pam said she was feeling better, and thought she'd have a very light scotch. Jerry made her a very light scotch.

"Really," she said, "Amelia was brighter than any of us. Which is odd."

Jerry grinned for a moment, and then said that Amelia Gipson had been very bright.

"Also," Weigand said, "she was prying. She went into things—particularly when she thought people were misbehaving. She had a very suspicious mind. And she jumped at conclusions—as I imagine she did in Spencer's case, the poor devil. She thought in this case that somebody had married her dear friend for her money chiefly, perhaps, because she really preferred to think the worst of people. Everything fitted when she got the idea that Burt was Purdy, but she was still guessing."

"And we," Pam said, after a pause, "just guessed all over the place. About the niece and nephew. About the perfume. About Mr. Spencer." She paused again. "What about him?" she asked.

"Just drunk," Weigand said. "Drunk—and unhappy. And in the wrong place at the wrong time." He considered. "As, probably, he always will be," he said. He lifted his drink, his eyes distant.

"He is one of the things—exposed—by all this," he said. "As always happens. Murder cuts across the face of things; the investigation of murder cuts again. We lay things open. By accident. We bring a man like Spencer out of the safe numbness he was living in; out of the safe obscurity. We find out something we don't need to know—don't want to know—about a girl like Nora M. Frost. We find out—"

Pam broke in. She spoke softly.

"What about Nora?" she said. "Was it what . . . I guessed? That she was afraid Miss Gipson would tell her husband?"

Weigand did not answer, in words. But his silence was an answer.

"But that's silly," Pam said, "because she'll tell him herself, I think. Whatever it was." She looked at Bill Weigand and then, because his expression seemed to contradict her, she nodded. "She'll think she shouldn't," Pam said. "She'll think it—it isn't fair. But she will. I'm pretty sure she will." She looked at Jerry, this time. "Women do," she told him.

He smiled at her and said, "All right, Pam."

"Well," she said, "they do. They can't not, even when they try."

"All right, Pam," Jerry said again. They looked at each other and after a moment Jerry smiled.

"It's a very consoling thought," he told her. "I'll keep it in mind, Pam."

Pam made a face at him, and then winced, because making a face hurt. She dropped that, and turned to Weigand.

"What did we do, really?" she said. "Except Mullins?"

Bill Weigand shrugged.

"Kept the pressure on," he said. "Looked into things. Asked questions. Made people nervous—and finally, made a murderer nervous. It happens that way. We asked questions, dug into things, fished around in the past—and one of us remembered something. He could—feel us around him, all the time. Pushing. He never knew when we'd find something—or what we'd find. So he couldn't simply stand by any more and merely watch. He had to try to find out what we were up to. He had to talk too much—to you, Pam. He had to kill too much. He had to break into your office, Jerry, to find out whether there was anything in Miss Gipson's notes which would incriminate him. Because we, like Miss Gipson, were prying into things."

"In all directions," Pam pointed out. "In too many directions. All of us—including you, Bill."

Bill agreed. He said they always did. They pried in all directions; eventually they got a break. Or, as in this instance, two breaks—Purdy's fear that Pam had picked up his mistake of knowing too much; Mullins' identification of his photograph. One had solved the case; the other had, undoubtedly, saved the lives of Purdy's wife and Pam North.

"For which," Pam said, "we are properly appreciative. Very. Why did Purdy think somebody wouldn't recognize him?"

"He thought he had changed enough," Weigand told her. "His hair had gone entirely gray; he had taken to wearing glasses. He had changed a good deal—enough so that I didn't recognize him, although I'd seen his pictures. And there was a psychological twist to it—he had had a stammer which he was conscious of—which was, he realized, an identifying characteristic no one could forget. When he wanted to change himself he concentrated on that—and he concentrated success-fully. And I suppose it loomed so large—in his mind—that when he had finally eliminated that one tremen-dous thing he underestimated the things that still remained—the things Mullins spotted—the set of the eyes—the shape of the face—all the things which, if you have a memory for faces, you don't forget. Mul-lins has a memory for faces."

"Still, Pam said, "it was risky."

Bill Weigand agreed. It was risky. Purdy had real-ized that. He had, he had told them when he began to talk, tried to avoid coming back to New York. But his wife had insisted—insisted so strongly that he was afraid if he did not agree, he would make her suspi-cious. Under the circumstances, he was, naturally, very anxious not to do anything which would alienate her. And—always—he thought he was changed enough. Bill finished with that and returned to his drink.

Pam spoke reflectively after a moment. She said they had certainly picked up a lot of miscellaneous information in their prying. Bill agreed again.

"Nora's secret," Pam said, "which Jerry and I aren't supposed to know about. The fact that Nora's brother needs money. All those things about poor Mr. Spencer."

Bill nodded. He said you couldn't tell what was important unless you went to the trouble of finding out about it. Nora did have a secret; her brother did need money.

"Which," Jerry said, "he'll now get. And the result,

I suppose will be another gadget for the home. A newer gadget."

Bill Weigand supposed so.

"And the perfume," Pam said. "That was another wrong direction. Who did visit her, Bill? Who smelled?"

Bill Weigand looked surprised.

"Oh," he said, "that was Burt, all right. Purdy. He took a little atomizer in his pocket with some of the perfume his wife uses. He sprayed it around the apartment when he went to switch the packet of medicine for one of poison. He thought we'd decide it had been his wife—I suppose he thought there was a chance we—the law—might kill her and save him the trouble. He was a fool, of course. He always was, apparently. And so he thought we'd all be. He thought that, even if we didn't look at once for his wife, we would certainly look only for a woman. He's explained the whole thing to us, very proudly, on the whole."

"I don't know," Pam said. "It seems sort of clever to me. Like a good dodge."

Bill Weigand said it was, in one way, very clever. Very subtle.

"And," he said, "very unlikely to mislead a cop. Because a cop would either not notice it at all, or not pay any attention to it if he did. Because cops can't bother with things which are merely—anomalous. They haven't time. They have to keep the pressure on."

"Why did Amelia Gipson get a job in Jerry's office, when she didn't need to?" Pam asked.

Weigand shrugged. He said he hadn't the faintest idea. He said probably because she was bored doing nothing.

"Or," Jerry amplified, "thought it was immoral not to be working. I suspect she would have thought that."

"The poor thing," Pam said. "So—so sure—and upright—and anxious to have things orderly and right. Whether it was really any of her business or not."

She lifted the cat down and held it on her lap,

stroking gently. The little cat began to purr. It had a very loud purr.

"It ought to be a lesson to us," Pam said, as much to the cat as to anybody. "To keep our paws out of things, Martini. Not to think the worst of people. Not to be—too inquisitive. And not to go to people you think are murderers and tell them what we think. It will really be a lesson to us, won't it, Martini?"

"I doubt it," Jerry said. He went over and sat down on the edge of the sofa by Pam. He put his hand out toward one of hers. Martini leaped at the new hand. She bit it.